MINTA
Forever

BY JEAN CAMPION

S0-BYX-290

WESTERN REFLECTIONS PUBLISHING COMPANY®

Montrose, CO

To Tom

For forty years of support

And to my children:
Cathy Dale Dougharty
Terry Jean Stinson
Jerry Thomas Campion

ISBN-13: 978-1-932738-37-7
ISBN-10: 1-932738-37-1

First Edition
Printed in the United States of America

Cover painting and map by Catherine Dougharty

Western Reflections Publishing Company®
219 Main Street
Montrose, CO 81401
www.westernreflectionspub.com

CHAPTER ONE

The Decision

⊱◈⊰

Friday, May 2, 1919—I have decided to leave Edmund. The why is easy; it's the how that will be a problem. I know he will not let go easily. In fact, I know he will not let go at all. I will have to leave secretly and silently and break all ties with this place and with my family. I have already tried writing to my parents. My mother's reply said I should try to be a "more obedient wife" and that I would "learn to love" Edmund. She didn't say how I could learn to love a man who enjoys hurting me and cares for nothing except his own desires. My parents don't understand that things are as bad as they are—it's so far from their own experience. I know there is no help in that quarter. The only one I can trust is cousin Lulabelle, but Edmund doesn't allow me to visit her or her to visit me. I must find a way to see her alone, as soon as possible. If I can't physically escape Edmund soon, I fear I will never be able to. I am still losing weight, and it's getting harder and harder to get all my work done on time—his time, of course, which makes him even madder at me. It will be a race to see if I waste away or if he kills me first. There have been several times when I feared he might.

Since I can no longer freely communicate with my darling Lulu, if I didn't have you to talk to, diary, surely I would go mad. My time with you today grows short. I must replace you in your hiding place. I will close, for now.

Ella Jane Morgan Skraggs put her diary back into its hiding place behind a loose board in the outhouse siding. She was sure Edmund wouldn't find it there. He didn't know the board was loose, and she was always careful to tightly replace the nail she had to remove. He would be home from town soon. She would have to hurry to have his dinner on the table, all of it hot, just the way he liked it.

When she heard the clomp of hooves and the jingle of the wagon harness, she was just taking up the fried chicken. She put the white meat pieces on his plate and one chicken leg on hers. Once she had tried taking part of one breast for herself and received a beating. He had informed her that white meat was for men. Women and children could only have dark meat. Apparently that was another "rule" she had failed to learn when she was a child. He was always complaining about how inadequately she had been raised. And he saw it as his job to correct her failings when he found them. Maybe if the age difference between them weren't so great—he was twenty-nine to her nineteen—he wouldn't see himself as her corrector.

She debated about dishing up the potatoes and gravy, but she decided to watch out the kitchen window and wait until she actually saw him coming from the barn. It wouldn't do to have them get cold on his plate. He didn't like food too hot, either. She shuddered as she remembered what had happened when he'd burned his lip on some soup. She set the fresh bread she had made earlier on the table; it should be all right, at least.

Edmund entered the kitchen and crossed to the wash bucket, his boots leaving a trail of mud she would have to clean up. There was a rug he could wipe his feet on, but he never did. At least the rest of his clothes were clean, as he had just gone to town and not worked in the barn or fields. She silently dished up the rest of the dinner and set the two plates at opposite ends of the table. She was thankful it was long enough that she wasn't in arm's reach of him while they ate. He liked to punctuate his corrections of her with arm-wrenching jerks, and his fingers left bruises in the soft flesh of her upper arms. He was usually careful to leave bruises only where they didn't show under her clothes. Of course, that meant only her hands and face were safe.

Not that it mattered. She wasn't allowed to go anywhere or see anyone, except for church on Sundays. He went with her once a month—

just often enough to maintain the fiction of being a God-fearing man. At first he only allowed her to go with him, but some ladies had come calling to see why she wasn't in church. Since then he allowed her to take the buggy the two miles into town every Sunday, but he knew exactly how long it should take her to get there and back. He didn't let her leave the house until the last minute, which meant she usually had to slip quietly into the back pew after the first prayer had started. She had overheard some women talking about how disorganized she must be because she could never get to church on time.

Then, when the service was over, she had to hurry home. Edmund waited on the porch, his pocket watch in his hand. Once, the minister went over his usual time. Of course, Edmund didn't believe that, and she had bruises and welts for a week. The next time that the minister talked too long, she got up and left, causing shocked looks and gasps. If anyone tried to talk to her after church, she had to make some excuse and leave. Finally, they quit trying to talk to her. She knew they thought she was standoffish as well as disorganized. But she kept going to church. It was the only time she was allowed to go out alone. The words of the sermon were often a comfort. And she loved the music—that most of all. She had been the pianist for their little church back home before she went to Normal School. She didn't have a piano in Edmund's farmhouse. When she had asked for one, he said music was frivolous and a waste of time.

Church was her only link to the world outside Edmund's 180 acres—that and the few letters she received from her parents in northern Indiana and Lulabelle in Abottsville, a day's buggy drive northwest of them. They lived near the little town of Lifton in west-central Indiana where Edmund was raised and where his church was. Edmund had grown up on the other side of Lifton, but his older brother inherited that farm. Edmund used his inheritance money to buy a farm from an elderly uncle who was dying of consumption. Edmund had built up the once run-down place into the successful corn and hog farm it now was. He also had a cow for milk and a chicken house. The cow and chickens had become Ella's responsibility as soon as she moved into Edmund's house.

He went into Lifton once a week to buy the supplies they needed and conduct whatever business he had. He never took her along. She hoped he had brought news or mail from town but knew better than to ask. She couldn't put the first part of the escape plan she was formulating into action until she had some mail. She nibbled at the small portions on her plate. She'd always been thin for her height—tall for a woman—but the past year had left her downright skinny. She just couldn't eat much without becoming sick. Her stomach was always tied in knots. Her once shiny, honey-colored hair had grown dull and coarse, too. Edmund had accused her the other day of deliberately letting herself go just to spite him.

Edmund ate in silence, without complaint. That was good. It meant she had done everything "right" this time. Maybe he would be in a good enough mood to share whatever he'd learned in town. He was a foot taller than she was and broad in the shoulders. She had thought him handsome with his brown hair and matching eyes when she first met him at the Indiana State Fair two summers ago, flattered that an older man was paying so much attention to her. Now she wondered why she'd ever found him attractive. She was only seventeen when she met him, but she was halfway through Normal School already since she'd skipped a grade and graduated from high school early.

"Would you like more potatoes, Edmund?" she asked, trying to keep her voice neutral. He often read things into the inflection of her voice. The simplest utterance could set him off on one of his rampages. She interpreted his grunt as affirmative and rose to serve him.

"I brought some mail," he said.

"Oh?" she replied, her heart racing. Mustn't act too eager. "Who could be writing to us?" No one wrote to Edmund, she knew. His people, although they had done well as farmers, couldn't write. But he considered anything of hers to be his, too, so she was careful to say "us" instead of "me."

"Probably that worthless cousin of yours, who else? No one else we know would waste time writing."

"Of course, cousin Lulabelle. I hope everyone's all right there." She deliberately planted the idea of not-rightness in his mind.

"*Lulabelle,*" he snorted. "What a stupid name for a stupid, frivolous woman." He had only met her once, at their wedding, when he was still trying to appear to be a decent man who was a "good catch" for her, as her parents said. He had certainly been charming to them, convincing them to trust their only child to someone so much older than she was. Sometimes she still couldn't believe how she'd been led to marry him against her hesitation.

After graduating from Central Indiana Normal School, the two-year teacher's college at Lagoda, she'd thought about applying for a teaching position out West which she saw an advertisement for, but her parents had said that teaching was only for widows and other women with no other alternative. They thought she should accept the proposal of the successful farmer from downstate who had met them at last summer's state fair in Indianapolis and courted her as much as possible since.

The school frowned on men visiting the students there, so she had only seen Edmund on her breaks from school, which she spent at home, and on two weekends when he came to Lagoda and met with her secretly. Back then, she'd been thrilled that a man would go to all that trouble for her, arranging to meet off-campus and taking her to dinner at the best hotel in Lagoda. Another student had even seen them once, but she thought the man was Ella's father. Ella didn't correct her friend since her own father was almost as old as a grandfather. And she didn't want to try explaining Edmund to anyone there. He had been her secret. And now her life with him was a secret—a secret so shocking that none of her genteel relatives would believe it.

At their clandestine meeting in Lagoda, he had held the door for her as they entered the dining room and pulled out a chair at the table for her, caressing her shoulder as he slid her into her place. He ordered the most expensive meal, saying, "Nothing but the best for you, darling."

She smiled into his dark brown eyes and felt so protected by him. He was attentive to her every word, frowning only when she talked of how much she enjoyed her classes.

"That's fine, to do well in your classes," he said. "But you won't ever need to work for a living as my wife."

Her heart did a little flip-flop. This was his first mention of marriage to her, and he made it sound as if it had already been decided.

"But I think I'd make a good teacher," Ella said. "I really like the students I'm working with now, and I know . . ."

"It wouldn't look right," Edmund said abruptly. "The man supports the family. The woman takes care of the man and gives him children. That's how God ordained it."

She fell silent. She couldn't argue with God. And the man across the table from her was so confident-looking, so in charge, so successful. She would be a fool to discourage a man of means, as he was.

She realized now Edmund had gone to the fair deliberately looking for someone—a naive girl he could sweep off her feet with the charm he could turn on and off at will. He had followed the family around as they listened to the politicians' speeches and looked at exhibits, then he approached them to ask her mother's opinion about the canned peaches.

"Excuse me, ma'am," he'd said. "But you look like an expert at canning. Do you favor a heavy syrup or light syrup for peaches?"

"Oh, you need heavy, for peaches," her mother said. "They turn dark, otherwise—like that jar that didn't get any ribbons." She pointed at the offending jar of peaches, shaking her head in disapproval.

He impressed her father by quoting from one of the speeches about the history of the fair: "To make two blades of grass grow where one had formerly grown, to increase crop yields, to preserve the soil fertility is a very worthy and sacred duty," by former Governor J.A. Wright. That's when he let the family know of his own successful farm and his blue ribbon exhibit of field corn.

Edmund ignored Ella until he had thoroughly impressed her parents with his knowledge of all things related to farming and with descriptions of his own farm. Then he suggested they all eat together at the booth in the pavilion. Things happened quickly after that. Much too quickly. He began calling on her parents regularly, even though it was an overnight drive for him to get up to their place. And he made those trips to Lagoda to see her.

Shortly after their dinner in Lagoda, Edmund asked her father for her hand, and it was given. Her parents planned a June wedding. She found out about it when she returned home after graduation, just two weeks before her wedding day. Edmund never asked her, just assumed she would want to be his bride. She said to her mother, "It's all so fast. I'm not sure I love him."

Her mother laughed her short, sarcastic laugh, more like a bark than a laugh. "Do you think I loved your father when we married? I was only sixteen, and I hardly knew him. But he was a good catch, as is Edmund. You'll grow fonder of him as the years go by. Besides, if you go out West to teach, when would we ever see you? Edmund lives a good distance away, but not as far as that. At least there's train service between us. And don't forget how you've always wanted children. I'm sure you know by now you need a man for that."

That statement had been the extent of Ella's sex education from her parents. The rest of her information came from whispered conversations with other girls at school and seeing what the farm animals and dogs did when they were "in season." She went to her wedding bed woefully ignorant of what to expect.

So, ever the obedient daughter, she acquiesced and accepted the wedding as planned. Things continued to move quickly after that. Her "engagement," if one could call it that, lasted only long enough to finish planning the wedding and to pack her bags. Edmund had insisted they needed to be married before the summer farm work started up. And now, she might as well be out West—or even China, for that matter—for all the good it did her to be closer to her parents and

Lulabelle. She was a prisoner in Edmund's home, a slave to a man she hated. The man sitting across the table from her now.

Edmund still hadn't produced the letter. She wanted to shout, "Just give me the letter, you oaf," but she knew that would be a sure way to have him destroy it as he did anything he thought was too important to her. Once, he had thrown a book she was reading into the fire because he thought it was taking time away from her "wifely duties," as he called anything he wanted her to do for him.

Eventually, after wiping his greasy fingers on the freshly laundered and ironed napkin she had provided, he slid the letter from his pocket.

Her fingers itched, she wanted to snatch it so badly. She waited. Finally, after carefully scrutinizing the letter as if it might contain hidden dangers, he handed it to her and said, "Read it aloud."

She knew that was coming. It was addressed only to her, but nothing of hers was private. Although, she had a big advantage that he didn't know about, she hoped. She was sure that he couldn't read more than a few basic words. He'd had to drop out of school at a very young age to help on the farm after his mother died in childbirth. His father didn't care for schools, and Edmund and his brothers had never attended after their mother's death. Of course, he never would admit to not being able to read or write, so she helped him maintain the fiction, offering to read or write anything that came up. He could sign his name, at least.

He always asked her to read whatever came in the mail, claiming the light inside wasn't good enough for his eyes, although he could see the smallest detail of whatever she was doing. Once, he had criticized the stitches on an apron she was mending because they weren't as small and even as he thought they should be.

She had gotten very good at changing words or leaving things out as she read without making it sound like she was doing so. In fact, her marriage had turned her from the once happy, open and honest girl she'd been into a lying, conniving woman who hid her feelings and had dark thoughts of suicide, and worse. She had to escape.

Lulabelle's letters always started, "Darling Ellie," but Ella read aloud, "Dear Edmund and Ella," so that he wouldn't have a fit about not being included. She continued reading, changing the first paragraph that started "We hope you are well as we are here" to "I'm afraid I have very bad news. Your mother has come down with the flu and is very ill. You must go at once to help her, Ella." She paused and gasped, clutching her throat dramatically, then continued reading. "I know Edmund can't leave the farm this time of year, but I'm sure he will spare you for a few days to help your mother in her extremity." She didn't have to fake the shaking of her hands. She didn't think it would occur to Edmund to wonder why her own father hadn't written her or just come for her. And the big flu epidemic that had swept the country last year was still claiming many people. It wouldn't be surprising that her mother would come down with it.

She paused, trying to read and comprehend what Lulabelle had really written. Nothing important. Just news of her happy new marriage to a kind and loving man—a wedding Edmund hadn't allowed Ella to attend, saying her "services" were needed on the farm. She looked up to gauge Edmund's mood. His face was dark and angry. Anything that inconvenienced him made him angry.

She pulled her handkerchief from her bodice and dabbed at her eyes. All she was producing were crocodile tears, but he had risen from the table and turned his back to her.

"Why can't Lulabelle go take care of her?" he asked.

"Edmund! Lulabelle's just her *niece*. I'm her *daughter*. What would people say?" The last sentence had its calculated effect. What people might or might not say was very important to Edmund. It wouldn't do to give the appearance of not doing things "right." And it was "right" that a daughter would go to a mother's bedside.

"Let me see that letter," Edmund said, turning and snatching it from her hands, tearing the page. He frowned at it intently, nodding as if he were reading and comprehending. But she knew it was an act.

"There's two paragraphs," he said as he thrust the page back at her. "You only read one. What's the rest say?"

She pretended to read silently, then looked up. "She says I should take the first train to Abottsville I can, and then she and Frank will take me the rest of the way up to my folks' place. That will save some money (always an important factor to Edmund). She also says she and Frank are well, and she hopes we are, too. Oh, Edmund, I must go to my mother." Ella said a silent prayer asking for forgiveness for all the lying. She'd been doing a lot of both lately: lying and praying.

"All right. Get yourself together, and I'll take you into the train in the morning. Just be sure to leave me enough meals, and don't be gone more than two or three days. Your mother can either get well or die in that time."

Real tears sprang to Ella's eyes. If her mother were really sick, he wouldn't care if she got well or died, just so long as she did one or the other quickly. But then, she was planning to leave and never see her mother again. Well, it couldn't be helped. She had to learn to face life as a runaway wife. The other choice, staying here as she was, wasn't even a possibility. She knew what that would entail. She picked up their plates and turned toward the sink to hide her tears. Usually, when she cried, Edmund felt obliged to "give her something to cry about." He was very good at it.

But she didn't have time to feel sorry for herself. She needed to get several days' worth of meals prepared ahead for Edmund, pack for herself, and refine her plans. She'd be up all night. On the other hand, if she were up all night, Edmund couldn't . . .

But he did anyway. He came into the kitchen about 2 a.m. and dragged her to the bedroom to "claim his rights," as he called it, muttering about needing to make up for the coming nights without her. She tried to relax as he grunted on top of her, satisfying himself with no thought to her comfort. She'd learned if she relaxed it didn't hurt as much. At first, when he hurt her, she'd cried and begged him to stop and tried to pull away. She discovered he liked that. It made him more excited and more violent. Now, she didn't fight back or complain, but he liked to be rough and usually managed to hurt her, leaving bruises and, sometimes, blood. Her worst fear was that she would become pregnant before she could escape. Then there would be no escape. How could she possibly make a new life for herself with a baby? Especially his. If he knew she was expecting his child, he would go to the ends of the earth to find her and bring her back.

Fearing that doing so was a sin, she prayed that this night would not result in a new life begun. Once it had been her fondest dream to have a child; now it was her worst nightmare. Then she prayed to be forgiven. Again.

CHAPTER TWO

The Plan

Monday, May 5, 1919—*I'm on the train returning to Edmund. It's been a busy two-and-a-half days. I don't have time to record all I did in here, but my preparations are now made. I just have to wait until things fall into place so that I can make my final escape. When I showed Lulabelle the bruises (the ones I was willing to show) and convinced her how bad things really are, she wanted me to just leave now, but I can't do that. Where could I go? First, I must have a place to go. And if I leave now, Edmund will go directly to Frank and Lulabelle, and who knows what he will do to them to make them tell where to find me? No. I must be far away in a place he will never look before he knows I'm missing. And he must not think anyone I know is involved. I thought about trying to stage my death, but I need to take certain items with me, so that charade would soon be uncovered.*

On the train on the way up, I thought of my new name. I have always fancied the name Minta. "Minta Morgan" has such a nice ring to it. But, of course, I can't return to my maiden name. I need something entirely different. I closed my eyes, and when I opened them again, the first thing I saw was the newly green fields of central Indiana rolling by. Such a peaceful scene: calm and peaceful and safe—like I want my life to be.

That's when it came to me. It's the month of May and the fields are green and beautiful. From now on I will be Minta Mayfield. Well, not quite from now on. First, I have to go back and be Ella Jane Morgan Skraggs for a while. But I will keep Minta in my heart and get her out whenever I can. Soon. Soon, I will be Minta forever.

In the lavatory of the train, Ella secreted her diary inside her bloomers, tightening the tie above her left knee so the small book couldn't slip out. It had been a big risk taking it along, but she wanted it with her to record her thoughts and plans. Edmund would meet the train, drive her home, and search her belongings to make sure she wasn't bringing back anything he didn't approve of, like magazines or a novel. He had even burned the collection of teaching magazines she'd accumulated at school, saying, "All magazines are the work of the devil" and that she had no further need for teaching materials anyway. He'd never actually searched her body, but part of what kept her on edge all the time was never being sure what to expect from him.

At least she'd been able to leave her other documents behind with Lulabelle, the ones she'd kept carefully folded in the back of her diary since her marriage. She smiled as she remembered the pleasant afternoon she and Lulabelle had copying them on the nice paper they'd purchased at the stationery store. First, they had copied her graduation certificate from the Normal School that said she was qualified to teach and then the letter of recommendation from Professor Kellogg. What a fit he'd have if he knew she had copied his hand and changed her name in the document! She just hoped that her references would be accepted at face value wherever she ended up and that nobody would check them. If employers inquired at her school or to Professor Kellogg about a Minta Mayfield, they would come up blank. But everything in the forged documents, except her name, was true, including the glowing recommendation the professor had given her.

He had written, *Miss Morgan is of the finest moral character, very well suited to handle a classroom of students. She completed the full two year course in pedagogy for common school teaching (1st-8th grades). She was at the top of her class scholastically, excelling especially in Latin, Grammar, and Composition. I recommend her for any teaching position without hesitation* . . . and so on. He tended toward wordiness, something she would correct if he were her student. She smiled at the idea. *I'm already thinking of myself as a teacher,* she thought. *Please, God, let it happen.*

In her hand was the last document she'd taken with her. It was time to destroy it. It could give Edmund a clue to her whereabouts if her plans came to fruition. And she didn't need it any more, now that the application letter had been sent. The newspaper ad that had been folded with the rest of her papers in the back of her diary since the day she agreed to marry Edmund, instead of applying for a teaching position, was worn and beginning to tear at the folds. She read it one last time: **Teachers Wanted: Strong unmarried women of good virtue for positions in one room schools in southwestern Colorado. Must be willing to live the frontier life. Contact Matthew Post, Superintendent of Schools, Liberty, Colorado.**

"Whatever does that mean," Lulabelle had asked, "willing to live the frontier life?"

"I don't know. Probably means am I willing to carry water and clean the outhouses," Ella answered.

"Yes. And able to saddle and ride a horse," Lulabelle added.

"And kill and dress my own meat. And face down attacking lions and bears." Ella was enjoying thinking of "frontier" items.

"And the snakes. Don't forget the snakes," Lulabelle shivered. "And wild Indians."

"Lulabelle! You know there are no more wild Indians. In fact, there was an Indian student at Normal School with me. They're just like us now."

"No they're not! What an idea! Especially out West. Our Indians are much tamer. But, seriously, Ellie—oops, sorry, I mean 'Minta.' Are you sure you can handle a life like that?"

Ella laughed bitterly. "Thanks to Edmund, I'm used to hard work, handling horses, dealing with outhouses—all of it. If I can handle life with him, I can handle anything the West has to offer, including snakes. In fact, a snake in my bed would be a welcome change from Edmund."

Lulabelle laughed. "Oh, Ellie. I'm going to miss you so much. You must find a way to let me know where you are and how you are."

"I haven't even been accepted yet. This ad is over a year old now. What if they don't need any more teachers?"

"I'll bet they always need teachers. Most of them probably don't last a year under whatever those frontier-life conditions are."

"Well, I will. And I told you I have to make a clean break. I can't write you, or anyone. Edmund might try to find me by stealing your mail."

"Oh, really, Ellie!"

"I'm serious. He'd do that. And worse."

Lulabelle frowned. "I have an idea. What if you write to my friend Constance, then, instead of me? Edmund has never heard of her. She can pass messages on to me and I to your parents, once they find out you've gone. That should be safe, and we'll be ever so much happier knowing you are all right."

Eventually Ella agreed to a plan whereby she would write to Constance when she could mail letters from a place not exactly where she lived. They even made up a code. Oregon would mean Colorado. Missionary work would mean teaching, and so forth. Lulabelle liked the intrigue of it all, not really grasping how deadly serious the whole thing was.

Ella stepped out onto the platform between cars on the train and opened her fist. The crumpled ad flew away, quickly gone from sight. "Go west," Ella whispered, referring to the application letter she'd sent to Colorado yesterday. "Bring me the answer I want."

As expected, Edmund was waiting impatiently at the train depot, acting as if the train's ten-minute tardiness was her fault. He grabbed her suitcase with one hand and her arm with the other.

"Come on," he said. He held her arm possessively, squeezing and digging in with his fingers. To a bystander, it would look as if he were merely helping her along as he pulled her roughly, his fingers digging in painfully when she didn't hurry fast enough for him. She had to walk carefully to keep from dislodging the diary in her bloomers. "It's time for chores at home. Work doesn't stop needing to be done just because you go galavanting all over the state." He didn't ask how her mother was, saving her another lie but hardening her resolve to leave him.

Once home, however, all thoughts of chores fled his mind. As soon as they were in the house, he pulled her roughly to him, one hand reaching for the clasps of her bodice, the other tugging at the waistband of her skirt. The diary felt heavy and awkward against her leg. He would find it in a minute.

"Edmund," she gasped, twisting away from him. "Please. I must visit the outhouse first. It was a long train ride."

"I suppose you were too hoity-toity to use the one on the train?" he said gruffly. "All right, but don't be long about it. I've waited about as long as a man can be expected to wait."

Fortunately he didn't follow her there, and she was able to secrete the diary back in its hiding place, waiting for another day—a day when Minta could come forward to rescue Ella.

CHAPTER THREE

Waiting

༻ঔৣ༺

Thursday, May 29, 1919—*Only time for a brief note. I wish the light were better in here. What a place to write—an outhouse. I'm afraid you will always smell like an outhouse, dear diary. Well, I hope it won't be for much longer. I know it takes a long time for mail to go all the way to Colorado and back, but I'm very impatient. What if they don't need anyone, and I never receive an answer? How long should I wait? What should I do if this plan doesn't work? I need another plan, but I've exhausted all my resources.*

The "good" news is that Edmund has been very restrained all week. At first I thought my absence had made him appreciate me a little bit, but now I think he's up to something. This morning I clumsily spilled a whole cup of coffee, and some of it splashed up onto his leg. He jumped up from the table, cursing, and I waited for the blows to begin, but he didn't touch me—just stomped out of the house. Later, I saw him kick that poor dog of his. Why it doesn't run away, I'll never know. If I could, I'd take it with me when I leave for a better life.

Oh, I so hope I get a letter from Lulabelle soon. At least my prayers have been answered for another month; I am not with child. If I didn't have you, diary, to talk to, I think I would go mad. Soon, Minta, soon we will be on our way.

The next morning Ella figured out why Edmund had been less aggressive than usual all week. When she heard the kitchen door open, she turned from the sink and found him setting the washtub by the stove.

"What are you doing, Edmund? It's not Saturday until tomorrow."

"Heat some water, woman. Bathe yourself. I made an appointment for you this afternoon with Doc Watters."

"Whatever for? I'm feeling fine. Oh! Are you afraid, because of my mother? But I don't feel like I'm coming down with the flu."

"Stop your stupid blathering. I'm not afraid of you catching what your mother had. But it's been almost a year now, and you still aren't with child. You should have provided me a son by now. I want to know what's wrong with you."

So he hadn't forgotten their anniversary was coming up. She certainly hadn't mentioned it and had wondered if he even remembered.

As she bathed, he watched her intently, and she realized he was looking for bruises or other signs of his abuse. So, that's why he'd been restraining himself. He didn't want the doctor to see any evidence of how he treated her.

As they waited in the front room of Doc's house for him to finish with another patient, Ella considered her position. She had seen Doc around town and at church, of course, but hadn't had occasion to visit him. He looked nice enough, but around here, everyone had known Edmund's family for years. In fact, Doc had treated three generations of them. She was the stranger. Who did she think people would believe if it came to a case of what she said versus what Edmund said? While Edmund and his brothers didn't seem to have any close friends locally, they were well-respected farmers and their opinion was sought on matters relating to crops and livestock. People would think badly of her before they would of him. She already knew that from the whispers about her she heard at church.

She stiffened as Doc's wife opened the door and called for her to come in. Edmund grabbed her elbow, and they rose together and started for the door. Doc appeared in the doorway and said, "Just you, Mrs. Skraggs."

"I'm her husband. I'm coming in with her," Edmund protested.

"Now, Edmund. This kind of exam is very, well, embarrassing for a woman. I'm sure she'd like a little privacy."

"She hasn't got anything I haven't seen before. And I want to know what's wrong with her."

"Be that as it may, I will not do the exam with you there. Now sit down and read the paper," Doc said as he pointed to the couch. "We'll be done in a few minutes. Then I'll talk to you and answer any questions you have."

Edmund grudgingly sat down. Ella had never heard anyone talk to him that forcefully. He often complained that his father criticized him all the time and ordered him around, expecting instant obedience to any command. She had never met his father, since he died a few weeks before their wedding.

Ella sat nervously in the chair Doc pointed to, thankful he didn't make her undress and sit on the examining table right away. She had no idea what kind of "embarrassing" exam he had in mind, but it couldn't be any worse than some of the things Edmund did to her. She had only seen a doctor for childhood illnesses and once when she broke her arm, falling out of a tree she wasn't supposed to climb. How would a doctor check her to see why she wasn't pregnant?

She knew she was blushing, and when she looked up, he was staring at her. At least his eyes looked kind.

"Mrs. Skraggs," he started.

"Please," she said, "call me Ella."

"Ella. Do you think something is wrong with you?"

"Why, no. I feel fine."

"I mean, something to make you not able to conceive a child? Do you have any problems with your monthly cycle or pain in your . . . you know . . . ?" He looked down at her lap. "Does it hurt when your press on your abdomen? Do you feel any lumps there?"

"No. No problems like that. No pain," she said, her face coloring again. What would he do if she added, "except the pain Edmund causes there"? But she didn't. It was too risky.

"Are your relations normal?"

"Yes. None of my relatives have had trouble having babies."

Doc stifled a laugh with a cough, his hand covering his mouth. "No, I meant your marital relations, with Edmund, in bed. Are you two doing what it takes to conceive a child regularly?"

She blushed again, more deeply this time. "Oh, yes, we're trying." Well, it was only half a lie. Edmund was trying. She was praying he wouldn't succeed.

"Yes, that's what I thought. Ella, I'm going to tell you something I promised Edmund's father I would never tell. I tried to get him to release me from that promise when I knew Edmund was getting ready to wed, but he refused. When Edmund was about fifteen, he caught the mumps. It was a nasty outbreak. I lost two young patients that winter. Sheldon Skraggs almost waited too long to call me out to his place. Edmund had it real bad. By the time I saw him, it had gone down on him. I told Sheldon there was a good chance that, if Edmund survived, he'd be impotent—do you know what that means?"

She nodded, her eyes wide, processing this new information.

"Sheldon threw a fit. Said I was never to say that to anyone ever again, especially to Edmund. Said that was something a young man should never hear about himself. Made me promise never to tell anyone and implied I was incompetent. Well, I knew someday Edmund would marry, and I hoped maybe I was wrong. It doesn't always cause impotence. I'm so sorry, Ella."

"Oh, that's all right. It's not your fault."

"I know how important having children is to a young couple like you. Maybe if you . . ."

She wanted to change the subject, partly to hide how happy she was about what he had told her. "What did you mean when you said the mumps 'went down on him'?" she asked.

It was Doc's turn to color, but he answered, "Well, it means the disease traveled from the glands in his neck to . . . another part of his body . . . and got into . . . affected . . . the part that makes the sperm."

"I see. So you're saying he doesn't have any . . . sperm?"

"No. He's got some. It's just not healthy like it should be. I don't know. He may have some good sperm in there, along with all the bad. Hard to tell, really. There's still a chance he could father a child. Maybe someday there will be a test we can do . . ."

She didn't want to think about what a test like that might require. "Are you going to examine me now?" she asked. She wanted to get it over with, whatever it was.

"I don't think I need to, considering what we've talked about," he said. "If you ever feel like you have a problem, I'd be happy to, but like I said, I think this problem is Edmund's. Would you like me to tell him, or will you do it? It's time he knew, even if Sheldon does flip-flops in his grave."

"No!" Ella jumped up. "I could never tell him something like that. Don't you tell him, either! His father was right—that's something he should *never* know." She couldn't imagine how angry such knowledge would make Edmund or what he would do to vent that anger.

Doc frowned, but something in her intensity told him not to press further. He stood and opened the door for her. "Well, I've got to tell him something. He's waiting out there to talk to me."

"You said there could be a slight chance he might be able to father a child. Just tell him to be patient and wait a little longer." All she needed was to buy some more time. "Tell him there's nothing wrong with me. And, maybe you could tell him . . . ," she hesitated.

"Yes, what is it? What do you want me to tell him?"

She took a deep breath, daring to trust this doctor just a little bit. "Maybe you could tell him not to try . . . to, to conceive . . . quite so hard and so often . . . ?"

Doc laughed. "He's a little too enthusiastic for you, is he? That'll wear off as he gets older. Sure, I'll tell him."

The buggy ride home was strained. Edmund ranted and raved about the doctor and his fool ideas and his charging an outrageous sum for doing absolutely nothing. Finally, losing her patience despite herself, she said, "What did you expect him to do? Wave a magic wand and produce a child?"

Edmund jerked the reigns and stopped the horse in its tracks. He turned to her, his eyes dark and narrowed. He raised his hand and slapped her across the face. "Don't you take that sarcastic tone with me," he said coldly. They rode the rest of the way in silence. She didn't cry. She was getting very good at not crying.

So the reprieve was over. He was no longer concerned about leaving marks. Why hadn't she asked the doctor to say he needed to see her once a week for "treatments"? Then Edmund would have to keep her free of bruises. But that would have meant telling everything to the doctor. She could tell no one, not here where she was the outsider.

She was back to waiting, tiptoeing around Edmund, trying not to provoke him. She was getting better at it, but every once in a while some new thing would come up that would set him off. Then she would add it to her mental list of what was not safe to do or say.

Doc, apparently, had talked to Edmund as he promised. Edmund only forced himself on her in bed every other night now instead of every night, except during her monthly visitation, of course—a week she looked forward to. That was almost worse, because he seemed more intense and angry, thrusting as hard as he could, as if he could conceive a child by brute force. He only wanted children for free labor on the farm. She already knew that. She shuddered to think what kind of life a child of Edmund's would have.

Every week, as soon as Edmund left for his weekly trip to town, she flung herself to her knees and prayed that this would be the day that the letter came. She had always believed in prayer, but now even more so since her prayers not to conceive had been answered in such an unexpected and complete way.

Finally, in early July, that prayer, too, was answered. Edmund brought a letter from Lulabelle. Now that Lulabelle knew what was going on, Ella didn't have to change anything except the greeting as she read it aloud to Edmund.

Dear Edmund and Ella,

I hope you are well. We are the same here. I have interesting news from my friend you met at the train station while you were here, Ella, the one who wanted to go west to be a missionary. She received an affirmative reply. She is to make arrangements to travel to Oregon as soon as possible, taking with her bedding and household supplies to live in a partially furnished cabin there.

I am so happy for her that her lifelong dream is to come true. I wish you could visit me, but I know you are much too busy on the farm. Your mother is recovering slowly and sends her love. Affectionately, Lulabelle

"Huh!" Edmund snorted when she finished reading. "What a waste of paper and stamp. What do we care about some flighty woman wanting to go out West and save the Indians? Missionary, indeed. She's probably ugly as sin and thinks she can find a man out there. Only a desperate woman would be a missionary—or a teacher, for that matter. Maybe she'll find some Indian buck and become his squaw."

"Edmund, please," Ella said, her joy making her brave. "Don't be lewd."

"Lewd am I? You'll see lewd tonight in bed, woman."

Ella gritted her teeth to keep from replying. Now it was a week before he would leave again for a whole day and she could put her plan into action. No one but a desperate woman would be a teacher, he'd said. Yes, that described her. Desperate.

CHAPTER FOUR

Escape

❧❦❧

Thursday, July 10, 1919—*Oh happy day! All is in readiness. Providence has stepped in and given me an extra day. Edmund announced last night that he is making an overnight trip to purchase a new boar. He's hitching up the wagon now. That means I can take the buggy instead of the wagon, as I'd originally planned, which will bring in more money when I sell it. I can travel faster and more comfortably, and he won't know I've gone until tomorrow night when he returns.*

As soon as I hear him leave, I will fly to the house and pack what clothes will fit into the small carpetbag, along with my Bible and you, dear diary. Then I will fill the larger suitcase with what linens and household items I can fit in and my sewing kit. That's all I can carry by myself on the train. I'll just have to hope I have enough money left when I get there to buy whatever else I need. I can't very well carry cooking pots and dishes on the train, even though the letter said I should bring them. It pains me to leave behind all my wedding presents, but that can't be helped. At least I can wear grandmother's watch pin and my best clothes. It will seem strange carrying my heavy coat on the train in July, but I will need it come fall and winter.

I am leaving Ella behind in this putrid outhouse, my cursed, but welcome, refuge. When I step out, I will be Minta. Minta from now on.

Minta ran to the house as soon as she heard Edmund leave. No tender lovers' goodbye for them. He had already given her his instructions for the time he would be gone. He had planned a lot of work for her to do, knowing that would keep her from going anywhere or seeing anyone.

She got a perverse pleasure out of leaving the chickens he'd killed for her to pluck and clean and cut up in the middle of the kitchen table. By the time he returned, they'd be spoiled and drawing flies. The blood from the severed necks was already dripping down and congealing on the floor. She opened the kitchen window to allow more flies to get in. Edmund hated flies in the house. He said they were an indication of her poor housekeeping skills, never mind that they came from his pig pen.

The good quilt her mother had made for her wedding wouldn't fit in the suitcase. She'd take it along in the buggy and leave it with Lulabelle. She didn't want Edmund to enjoy its warmth any more. Only two changes of clothes fit into the carpetbag with her nightgown and under-garments. Her students would just have to get used to seeing her wear the same thing every day. Pay hadn't been mentioned in the letter, but she doubted it would be enough for a new wardrobe.

As she was loading her luggage into the buggy, she noticed the dog slinking along the side of the barn. She ran into the house and grabbed one of the chickens and threw it to him. "Get out while you still can," she yelled at the dog as she left. It ignored her, gulping the pieces of flesh that it was tearing from the bird.

The trip to Abottsville would have only taken a few hours by train, but it would take her most of the day to drive the buggy there. A few of the other local farmers had bought the new Model T automobiles, but Edmund, of course, said the old ways were the best and he would stay with his horses. But she had to drive the buggy to Abottsville, she couldn't go to the local train depot where she would be recognized. Besides, she didn't have money to buy a train ticket. She would have to be on the westbound train and out of Abottsville by tomorrow night. She hoped the note she left Edmund would delay his search for her a few days.

The note, pinned to the bed, read:

> *Edmund,*
> *After you left, a telegram was delivered. My mother is gravely ill. She is not expected to live. I took the buggy since I don't have any money for a train ticket. I will be back as soon as I can. Ella*

He would have to take the note to a neighbor and make some excuse about why he couldn't read it himself. Then the neighbor would know she had left and, when she didn't return, the gossip mill would run overtime. She laughed, thinking of the predicament she'd left him in.

The note was a thin ruse, but it was the best she could do. He would be furious—about the buggy and horse and especially her being gone without his permission, about the chickens, about all the chores left undone, about having to find someone to read him the note. Come to think of it, he probably would go all the way to his brother's rather than risk letting a neighbor know their business. His brother's oldest boy had gone to school for a while and could read.

Eventually, Edmund would look around the house, see what all she had taken, and suspect she wasn't planning to return. Once he looked in the cedar chest and saw her winter coat gone, he'd know for sure. She hoped he'd go first to her parents' place to look for her. They knew nothing, so they wouldn't have to lie, and they lived north while she'd be going west. Then he'd go to Lulabelle and Frank. Lulabelle knew how to lie, and Frank had been convinced to go along with their scheme by the bruises Ella had shown him on her throat and arms, as well as by his inherent dislike of Edmund the few times they had met. By the time Edmund got to Abottsville, she, Minta, would be long gone. Unreachable. She hoped.

She arrived in Abottsville without incident before dark, but she was too keyed up to sleep much that night. She and Lulabelle sat up talking as they had when they were younger and allowed to spend the night together. They reminisced mostly about their childhood and their time in school. Lulabelle was a year older than Minta, but Minta had skipped fourth grade, so they were in the same class from then on.

"What a strange turn our lives are taking now," Lulabelle said. "We may never see each other again." Her blond curls tumbled down over her eyes as she twisted the handkerchief in her hand.

"Yes, that's possible," Minta answered. "But you and Frank may take a trip out West someday. As for me, I'm never coming back."

"What about your parents? Don't you want to see them ever again?" Lulabelle's blue eyes misted over.

"Of course I do, but I had to decide. I had to decide to either stay here and wither and die with Edmund or go somewhere else and live. I chose life. I can't come back here. Ever. I wrote a letter for you to give my parents after I'm gone. I do love them, and I wish things could be different. I tried to explain everything to them in the letter."

It seemed strange giving Lulabelle a message about love to her parents. It was a word that had seldom been mentioned in their house as long as she could remember. She'd been well cared for as a child but never hugged or kissed. It just wasn't their way.

As soon as businesses opened in the morning, she, posing as a grieving widow who must sell her possessions, and Frank, posing as her brother, took the horse and buggy to a dealer and sold them along with the tack. Then he took her to a pawn shop and she sold her wedding ring. The proprietor eyed the watch pinned to her bodice and asked if she'd like to sell it, too. It was worth more than the wedding ring, he said. Typical of Edmund to find the cheapest wedding ring possible. She fingered the watch, remembering seeing her grandmother surreptitiously check it during sermons at church.

"No, I can't part with this," she said.

"Funny," the man answered. "Women usually have the most trouble giving up their wedding rings."

"Well, I wasn't married very long," she said, as if that explained it.

He shrugged and counted out the coins. All together she got enough money for the train ticket with a little left over for expenses on the way and, she hoped, a cooking pot and tea kettle, as well as other necessities for her cabin. To save money, she bought a ticket for Coach, rather than on one of the Pullman sleeping cars. She'd either sleep sitting up in the seat or not at all; it didn't matter.

Lulabelle packed a large picnic basket of food for Minta to take on the train. Minta had already refused to take any money from

Frank and Lulabelle, knowing they didn't have it to spare. They had already paid for her expenses applying for the job.

Lulabelle cried at the depot as Minta was getting on the train. "I will miss you so much. Please write to me. Please be safe and have a happy life."

"That's all I've ever wanted, Lulabelle, to be safe and have a happy life. Maybe now I can." Minta didn't cry until the train was moving and the two figures waving on the platform were getting smaller and smaller, fading away like her past life was. She pulled her handkerchief from her bodice and wiped her eyes. Resolutely, she turned forward in the seat and faced her future.

When she opened the picnic basket to eat lunch, she found coins amounting to two dollars that Lulabelle had secreted in a napkin, and her tears finally overflowed. It was such a luxury to cry unmolested that she indulged herself, not caring what others on the train might think. She had more than a year's worth of tears to cry. The conductor was the only one who commented. "It's always hard leaving loved ones behind, isn't it?" he said kindly as he walked through, checking the car. What would he think if he knew she was a runaway bride and that some of her tears were tears of joy and relief at leaving her husband behind?

After the confusion of changing trains at the new Kansas City Union Station—the Gateway to the West, as the sign proclaimed—Minta didn't remember much of the next twelve hours of the trip. She slept, her head resting on the carpetbag clutched on her lap, exhausted from her crying spell and from the frantic activity of the last two days. When she opened her eyes, it was dark. She tried to see something out the window, but the train was moving through almost complete blackness. Once in a while she saw, or thought she saw, a light far away. What a big country this was, to have so much space without even a house or train station.

She ate more of the food Lulabelle had packed and used the lavatory at the end of the car. By then it was getting light. She watched out the window as a seemingly endless expanse of prairie drifted by. Once in a while they'd cross small streams, many of them dry, some containing a trickle of water. Eventually, they stopped at a station. She asked the conductor where they were.

"Burlington, ma'am."

"What state?"

"Colorado. Burlington, Colorado."

Minta gasped. "We're in Colorado already?"

"Just the very eastern edge, ma'am. In a few more miles you'll be able to see the Rocky Mountains, but it's still a long way to Denver. That's the end of the line for this train."

"I know. I have to change to another train there. The Rio Grande South."

"Oh? That one goes through the mountains. Where are you going?"

"Durango. That's where I'm going on the train. Then I have to hire someone to take me to . . . ," she stopped, "to where I'm going." She'd have to remember to be careful. What if Edmund somehow found out what train she'd taken and talked to people who worked on it? The less anyone knew about her business, the better.

Ella had been an open and trusting person. Minta would have to develop a healthy skepticism about everyone and everything. Minta would have to be strong and brave. That's what she was counting on. Her life depended on it.

CHAPTER FIVE

The Arrival

Wednesday, July 16, 1919—*I had intended to write on the train, but first I was too tired, then it was too dark, and the last part of the trip was too interesting. I had not imagined the magnitude of the Rocky Mountains. I couldn't take my eyes off the scenes outside the window—ever-changing vistas of mountains with streams rushing along beside the train. The mountain ranges seem to go on forever and are so formidable. Surely Edmund can never find me hidden amongst them as I now am.*

We left Alamosa at 7:00 yesterday morning, stopped at little towns called Antonito and Pagosa Junction and arrived in Durango at 5:30. A man approached me at the station in Durango and asked if I was the "new teacher bound for Liberty." I wanted to say, "Oh, yes, bound for life, liberty, and the pursuit of happiness," but I just nodded. He explained Matthew Post had told him to look for a woman arriving alone and to tell her to go to the post office in the morning and catch a ride with the mail. So I didn't even have to hire a conveyance, but I did have to spend some of my money for a hotel room. The man told me about a little hotel several blocks away that was cheaper than the big, fancy Strater Hotel by the train station. It was good to sleep in a real bed after so long on trains.

Liberty turned out to be much farther than I expected and over a very rough road. Liberty is a bustling little mining town. New houses and businesses are being built in all parts of the town. I asked what was mined, and the driver said the gold and silver was about played out, but they'd just started work on a big deposit of coal nearby. The mail driver dropped me off in front of School Superintendent Matthew Post's shop, so I didn't even have to search out my employer. His office is just the back room behind his surveyor's shop. Apparently, his main job is locating property boundaries and making maps. I hope he will come talk to my students sometime. It seems like a fascinating business.

So much has happened since I walked into his office—signing the contract, shopping for supplies, spending the night with Mr. and Mrs. Post, being regaled with endless bits of advice about how to survive in a one-room school and its community. Mr. Post is to drive me to the school and my cabin today. I can hardly wait. First, we are stopping at the school here to pick up some supplies my school is being given. Hand-me-downs and rejects, I suspect, but I don't care. I would make do with a stick in the dirt, if that's all they gave me. I hear the wagon coming now. He said he could get his automobile only about halfway there, so we are taking a wagon. The next time I write will be in my own cabin, Minta's safe house.

Minta put her diary back into her bag and carried it to the door, where Matthew Post met her. If only all men could be like him, Minta thought. The years made some men mean and cranky, like Edmund; others, silent and withdrawn, like her father; and some, like Mr. Post, wise and kind. She was sorry she would be so far away from his sage counsel when problems arose, as she was sure they would with her school.

He had told her about the four one-room schools in District 56: Halpern, Piñon Hollow, Shady Rest, and Rockytop. Halpern was taught by a man who had been there several years. Piñon Hollow's teacher was a widow who needed to support her family. The other two were still vacant. Matthew, as he insisted she call him, assumed she would want Shady Rest, because it was closest to town and easiest to get to.

"I don't know what we'll do about Rockytop," he said. "It's so hard to get anyone to go way out there, especially when they see the road."

"I'll take Rockytop," she said. "You can find someone else for Shady Rest."

"Are you sure? A young woman on your own? I warn you, there will be no social life, except for interacting with the families who live out there, and they're all busy trying to survive on some of the worst farm ground around. And there will be no way for you to get to town unless someone kindly offers to take you. The winter can be especially bad out there. There may be days or even weeks when you can't get to town, even if you have to." That sounded wonderful to her. It meant no one else could get out to her, either.

"That's all right," she said firmly. "I'll take Rockytop."

He frowned, studying her in silence for a while, then gave her the contract to sign. She had seen similar ones at Normal School, so she wasn't surprised by any of it. It read:

LIBERTY COUNTY TEACHER'S CONTRACT FOR 1919—
DISTRICT 56 ($60 A MONTH)
MISS (she signed "Minta Mayfield" with shaking fingers, making her lie real) AGREES

1. NOT TO GET MARRIED.
2. NOT TO KEEP COMPANY WITH MEN.
3. TO BE HOME BETWEEN THE HOURS OF 8 P.M. AND 6 A.M., UNLESS IN ATTENDANCE AT A SCHOOL FUNCTION.
4. NOT TO LEAVE TOWN WITHOUT THE PERMISSION OF THE CHAIRMAN OF THE BOARD.
5. NOT TO SMOKE CIGARETTES.
6. NOT TO DRINK BEER, WINE, OR WHISKY. THIS CONTRACT BECOMES NULL AND VOID IF THE TEACHER IS FOUND DRINKING BEER, WINE, OR WHISKY.
7. NOT TO DRESS IN BRIGHT COLORS AND TO WEAR AT LEAST TWO PETTICOATS.
8. NOT TO WEAR FACE POWDER OR PAINT THE LIPS.
9. NOT TO DYE HER HAIR.
10. TO KEEP THE SCHOOLROOM CLEAN
    A. TO SWEEP THE CLASSROOM FLOOR AT LEAST ONCE DAILY.

> B. TO SCRUB THE CLASSROOM FLOOR AT LEAST
>   WEEKLY WITH SOAP AND HOT WATER.
> C. TO CLEAN THE BLACKBOARD AT LEAST ONCE
>   DAILY.
> D. TO START THE FIRE AT 7 A.M.

"Does the man who teaches at Halpern have to wear two petticoats, too?" she asked with a twinkle in her eye as she handed Matthew the signed contract.

Matthew smiled. "No. We have a separate contract for men. It's just that most of our teachers are women, and many of them leave to get married before they even finish out their first year. I'm sure you understand."

"I do. And I won't do that, I promise."

"Don't make promises you might not be able to keep. As soon as word gets out that there's a pretty new teacher at Rockytop, you'll be surprised by the number of men who will suddenly find they've got business out there."

She couldn't imagine that she'd have trouble with any portion of the contract. She certainly had no interest in attracting or keeping company with men. In fact, the fewer men she saw, the better. And she had never indulged in any smoking or drinking vices or had any wish to change the honey color of her hair. Keeping the schoolroom clean would be a joy, not a chore, because it would be *her* place, and she liked her place to be clean, orderly, and cheerful. Edmund had insisted that the curtains remain closed at all times; she liked bright, sunlit rooms.

Matthew explained there was a back road—more of a trail, really—to Rockytop that was shorter, though not suited for a wagon. And they needed to take the longer route to go by Shady Rest. Even that road could only accommodate automobiles part of the way. Their first stop was the new, brick, four-room school in Liberty. It reminded Minta of the four-room school she had once attended. Her parents, however, had gone to one-room schools and talked fondly of their experiences there. Minta was glad she didn't have to share her school with any other teachers. It would make it easier to maintain her fiction.

She and Matthew filled the back of the wagon with old textbooks and other supplies the school was getting rid of. Some would be dropped off at Shady Rest on their way, and the rest would be hers to use as she saw fit. He handed her a wrapped package to carry on her lap and told her not to open it until she was setting up the school. He said it was probably the only new thing she'd get for her school this year, and he wanted her to have it. She got the impression he bought it with his own money. She restrained her curiosity after surreptitiously feeling it and determining it was something made of cloth.

Finally, they were on their way.

"Why is the school called Rockytop?" Minta asked. She nearly had to shout to make her voice heard above the creaking and groaning of the wagon on the road roughened by deep, dry ruts.

"You'll see when you get there," was all Matthew Post would say about it. But he had a lot to say on other subjects, mainly her need to fit in with and get along with the Rockytop residents. There were currently seven families in the upper Halpern Creek Valley served by Rockytop.

"The members of your school board," he told her, "are the president, Fred Haley, who's got six kids, but I think only four will be in school this year; Luke Woods, he's a widower with two kids; and Jens Fredrickson. His twins will be your biggest challenge, I'll wager, plus a couple of his grandkids will be in school in a year or two. Besides those families, there's Fred's sister-in-law and her two kids. Fred's brother died when his horse tossed him off awhile ago. And the Archuleta clan, they've got three or four girls and another on the way. Oh, yes, and the Valoris have one or two in school and little Joseph; he hasn't been right since he was born. He probably won't be going to school. And Old Man Rickerts lives out that way, 'course he doesn't have any kids."

"Wait, wait," Minta laughed. "You're going too fast. I'll never keep them all straight."

"It will take awhile. But I'd advise you to learn all the kids' names the first day. Things will go easier for you if you do. If I counted right, you'll have twelve or thirteen to start. Since we're still in the summer work season, some will be in and out until fall. But, like I explained, we usually have to take a month or two off in the winter, so we try to get some schooling done in the summer when we can. In fact, you can start as soon as you get the school and your cabin set up to your liking. Fred's place isn't too far from the school. Just walk over and let him know when you want to start, and he'll let everyone else know."

Their throats were sore and scratchy from trying to talk through the dust and over the creaking and groaning of the wagon wheels complaining about the road. They lapsed into silence, and Minta watched the piñon and juniper trees drift by as the wagon labored up and down several dry gullies. When they rounded the last corner, Rockytop came into view.

Minta gasped, "There it is! Rockytop! Oh, I see." What she saw was an odd jumble of rocks sitting on top of a rounded hill that rose several hundred feet out of the valley surrounding it. At the base of the hill was a once-white clapboard building that looked just like the Shady Rest School at which they'd stopped earlier. They were both situated so a row of windows along one long wall faced east. The two structures were so similar, Minta thought they must have been built from the same plans. An older, smaller log cabin, which was the teacherage, was just past the school. Two small outhouses were a ways behind the school, and a shed sat between the school and cabin. A mostly broken down log fence surrounded the schoolyard. But Minta's eyes kept being drawn back to Rockytop.

"I've never seen anything like it. It's, it's . . . ." She was at a loss for words.

"Yes, it's very unique," Matthew said. "Most of the schools out here are named to reflect their surroundings. Halpern is where Halpern Creek joins the Liberty River. Piñon Hollow is in a hollow full of piñon and juniper trees. As you saw, Shady Rest is under the cottonwoods along the road to town, and here's Rockytop."

"It's so interesting and beautiful. I must climb it."

"Wait until after a good freeze. There can be rattlesnakes up there this time of year. And don't let the kids climb it, at any time. That's one of the rules out here. There's a pretty steep drop-off on the other side."

"Are there any other rules I should know about?"

"Probably. Ask Fred. He's the main disciplinarian in this valley. His kids—or anyone else's, for that matter—will tell you so."

Oh, no, Minta thought. Is this Fred going to be another Edmund? She wasn't sure how she'd react to another man who thought he could ride roughshod over everyone around him.

Just up the valley from the school she saw a cluster of buildings that was someone's farm. As she watched, several children left what they were doing in a field and ran toward the house.

"Fred's kids," Matthew said. "They'll let everyone know we're here. By the time we're ready to unload the wagon, we'll have help."

They did. She was introduced to Fred Haley, a tall, muscular man in his forties, and his almost-as-tall son, Richard, who, on her inquiry, admitted to being seventeen and out of school. A younger boy, Michael, looked at her shyly out of the corner of his eye and pushed his even younger brother, Robert, forward to shake hands when she offered. Another boy, about thirteen, was introduced by Fred as "Angus Haley, my nephew." Angus barely acknowledged her, turning his back and starting to unload boxes of books from the wagon.

With that crew, it took only a few minutes to put all the supplies in the schoolhouse. Then they moved to her cabin and unloaded her few personal belongings. Even in such a small cabin, they made a pitiful pile in the middle of the floor. There was already a bed, cookstove (the only source of heat), and wooden table with two chairs. There were faded, grimy curtains at the two windows, but she thought she'd be able to make them presentable. She was anxious to get started and wished they'd all leave.

"We'll be having a meeting in the schoolhouse tonight," Fred said. "So everyone can meet you. You can tell us when you want to start school then."

She looked at Matthew with panic in her eyes. She wasn't ready to start yet!

"Good idea," Matthew said, smiling at her calmly. "That way I can stay for the meeting, and we can settle our regular school business, too."

"Claudia and Rachel will organize a potluck first," Fred said. "You don't need to bring anything, Miss Mayfield, seeing as how you just got here. How does 6 o'clock sound?"

Suddenly Minta realized she'd been asked a question. Miss Mayfield! It sounded so strange. She hadn't realized at first that he was talking to her; she'd have to get used to that name. She was used to calling herself Minta already, but not Miss Mayfield. It seemed she'd been Mrs. Skraggs for so long. How did one go back to being a Miss instead of a Mrs.? What was it he'd asked? Something about how 6 o'clock sounded.

It sounded like Fred was used to telling everyone what to do, but she didn't say that. She answered, "Fine. I'll see you all again at six." Thankfully, they all left her to her own devices, Matthew going along with Fred to discuss the agenda of the meeting. She left her own unpacking undone and went to straighten up the schoolhouse. They couldn't have dinner and a meeting there with boxes all over the floor.

Empty shelves lined the wall behind the teacher's desk. There was nothing along the wall whose windows faced east to catch the morning sun and bring in the natural heat. The wall opposite the windows held two long blackboards. She filled the shelves with the books she'd been given, without taking time to organize them, and stacked the boxes in the cloakroom. Matthew might want to keep them. If not, they'd make good fire starters when it got cold enough to need to use the wood stove that was in the middle of the floor near the back.

The teacher's desk was centered in front of the shelves with another blackboard above them on the wall opposite the door. She allowed herself a minute to stand and then sit behind it, running her hand along the smooth surface. It was hers, now. She could hardly believe it. Her hand came away black with dust. Well, she could fix that. She stood up and resumed work.

A flag pole with a faded and dusty flag stood in its stand next to the desk. She pulled the flag out straight to look at it and frowned. One of the old forty-six-star ones. Well, she'd just have to make sure that the students knew Arizona and New Mexico had joined the union, and there should be forty-eight stars.

Twelve student desks were bolted to the floor in three rows, with a bench for recitation in the front row. In the back corner a tall cupboard held various supplies, and she added those they'd just brought in. A few extra chairs were scattered around, but not enough for tonight's meeting. Even if they brought over the two from her cabin, some people would have to stand. And there was no electricity. What did they do about evening meetings? She only found one lantern. It would hardly make adequate light for such a large space.

But best of all, in the corner opposite the cupboard stood an old, upright piano. When the boxes were all empty and stored, Minta sat down on its bench, not even caring if her skirt got dusty. She was almost trembling, she wanted to play the piano so badly. But first she took the package Matthew had given her from where she'd put it on top of the piano. Laying it in her lap, she unwrapped the brown paper. Tears came to her eyes as she held up a brand new, forty-eight-star flag. It was almost as if Matthew knew, in some way she couldn't understand, what would be important to her. She rose and went to the flag pole. She removed the old flag and attached the new one. Then she didn't know what to do with the old one. She folded it carefully and set it on her desk. She'd ask at the meeting tonight what was to be done with it.

She went back to the piano and sat down again. She blew the dust off the keys and, holding her breath, began to play, softly at first, then louder and louder. It felt wonderful. The piano wasn't even too badly out of tune. She was pounding out and singing along to "The Battle Hymn of the Republic," when she realized she wasn't alone.

"Oh, don't stop, please," a golden-haired girl of about fourteen said. "Our last teacher could only play with two fingers, and not much with them. I'm Honor. My mother sent us to see if you could use some things. They're in your cabin. We didn't find you there, and then we heard the music, so we came over here. I wish I was still going to school here. But I passed the eighth grade exam and graduated last year. Father can't afford to board me in town, so I have to stay home this year. Maybe next year I can go to high school," she paused for a breath, allowing Minta to talk.

"I hope you can, Honor. You seem like a very smart girl who should go to high school. Maybe you could come help me sometimes this year."

"Oh, I'd love to. If mother can spare me from the house, that is. And if father will let me."

"And your father is?"

"Fred Haley," Honor said, as Minta expected.

Honor turned and called toward the cloakroom, "Mary, don't be shy. Come in here." A smaller version of Honor peeked around the corner and then eased her way into the room, looking rather intently at the floor.

"This is my cousin, Mary," Honor said. "She's ten and in the fifth grade."

"How do you do, Mary? My name is Miss Mayfield. I'm very happy to have you in my school."

Mary looked up and smiled shyly.

"Mary loves school, just like I did," Honor said.

Mary mumbled something Minta didn't catch. She looked at Honor questioningly, who then explained, "Mary says, 'not Angus'. Angus is her brother. He's thirteen. He doesn't like school. Sometimes he acts like a low-down ol' polecat. You'll probably have to beat him. Or else Father will."

"It's way too soon to be talking about beating anybody," Minta laughed. "Let's at least get to the first day of school." Her earlier exploration of the back cupboard had revealed a wooden ferule, a flat piece of wood with a handle, the type she remembered from her school days—not from personal experience, but she remembered some of the boys in her class being paddled with one. At the time, she thought that was a good idea. But then, she hadn't been the one holding the ferule. In her classes at Normal, some of the professors said they could see the day coming when corporal punishment would no longer be allowed in schools. Others laughed at that notion and said it would never happen, that chaos would result if it did.

One of the lectures Matthew had given her on the way out had been about maintaining discipline. When she had said she thought there were better ways to handle problems than with beatings, he said, "You'll do well to follow the standards of the community. If that's what the community expects of you, that is what it is your job to do." And now that she'd met the self-proclaimed head of the community, Fred Haley, she thought she knew what those standards would be. Well, it was her school, and she'd run it the way she saw fit. Brave words for a woman who can't afford to lose her job, she thought.

"Miss Mayfield?" Honor asked. "Can we go see about the stuff in your cabin? We have to get back to help with the cooking for the potluck. Oh, and we'll come a little early to sweep up the school. You won't have to do that."

"Thank you, Honor. That was going to be my next job. But I guess I do need to get myself cleaned up and ready, too. I was wondering if there are more lanterns somewhere. Won't we need more light tonight?"

"Oh, every family brings a lantern with them. Then there's plenty of light."

"You ain't needin' to fix yourself up. I've never seen such a purdy growed-up lady," Mary said, just barely loud enough for Minta to hear. She'd have to work with her on speaking up in school. And her grammar. Too bad Honor wouldn't be one of her students. She could be a great help.

"Thank you, Mary," was all Minta said this time.

Back at her cabin, Minta was overwhelmed at the pile of things the girls had brought. There was a quilt for the bed, faded and mended but still serviceable; two cooking pots of different sizes; dish towels; a pillow and two pillow cases; a lantern; and several boxes of home-canned food. Someone must have mentioned to Mrs. Haley how little she had brought with her.

"I can't take all this," Minta exclaimed. "Tell your mother she is too generous."

"She said she remembers what it was like moving here without a stick of furniture to her name," Honor said. "We lived in a tent for two winters. I can just barely remember the time before we got the house built. We spent almost all our time grubbing out sagebrush, so we'd have open land for a field. We still do. Whenever there's not other work to do, Father sends us out to grub sagebrush. I *hate* sagebrush. Anyway, mother knows you can use this stuff. And I'll bet the other families bring you more tonight. That's what we do out here. We all take care of each other."

"I think I'm going to like it here," Minta said, smiling. She didn't understand "grubbing out sagebrush," but she guessed it was one of the things she'd be learning soon. "You girls run on home now. I'll see you in a little bit. I'm glad I got to meet you both before all the people come tonight."

"We're glad, too, aren't we, Mary?"

Mary eased out of the door the way she'd come in, but she kept her face up this time, staring at Minta, her big, bluish-gray, trusting eyes the last thing visible as she disappeared around the corner.

CHAPTER SIX

Getting Started

꿍

Friday, July 18, 1919—*I'm sitting with my second cup of coffee at the table in my cabin. Yesterday I got the curtains washed and pressed. I had to buy an iron with my meager funds—it wouldn't do to go to school with my garments unpressed. My other indulgence was a good supply of Arbuckles' coffee. Mr. Post assured me it was the best available here. I am enjoying the sunshine coming in the east window and not having to jump up to do Edmund's bidding from the second I wake up. It's beginning to sink in that I'm really on my own now.*

It's also beginning to sink in that I have to start teaching in less than a week. We decided at the school meeting that for the first month I'll only have the younger students, 1st-3rd grades, as the older ones are still needed for farming activities. Then, in September, the 4th-7th graders will come, and all fourteen will be in attendance. I'm glad I don't have any 8th graders this year. I don't have to prepare anyone for the State Exam. But I have so much to do to get ready. I need to organize the books and materials to see what I have and what is lacking. And Matthew gave me the State Standards for each grade, so I'll know what I'm supposed to be teaching them. The school needs a thorough cleaning now that my cabin is mostly in shape. And I don't even want to think about the outhouses, but that has to be done, too. The shed, I discovered, holds a good supply of wood. Fred Haley told me to let a board member know when it's getting low and they'll refill it. He said they use wood instead of coal because it's free. Most of the farmers here are still clearing land for fields and cut more wood than they can use.

I'd like to write my first impressions of all the people at the meeting but that would take too long, and I know first impressions are often wrong. They almost all seemed very nice and acted as if they were trying to make a good impression on me, which made me feel funny since I was trying to make a good impression on them. I don't know if I succeeded or not.

Fred (everyone here insists I use first names instead of Mr. and Mrs.——even Matthew Post which seems strange, since he's so much older——but I'm trying to get used to it) made a big point of telling me, in front of his children, that if they got into any trouble at school they would be in twice as much trouble at home. Most of the rest of the fathers said similar things. Mrs. Fredrickson, Hannah, told me where to go by the stream to cut the best willow switches and said her boy and girl twins, Gunny and Gertie, would be in need of them frequently.

"I declare," she said, "what one of them two don't think up to get in trouble, the other one does." But she had a twinkle in her eye when she said it. She's old compared to the other mothers; the twins must have been change-of-life babies. I guess Matthew was right about the standards of the community. But I plan to have such well-organized and interesting lessons that my pupils won't want to get into trouble.

The only parents who didn't mention discipline to me were the Archuletas, and their little girls seemed so sweet and shy that I can't imagine them getting into trouble. Fred's wife, Claudia, told me after the Archuletas left that they really lived closer to Piñon Hollow School, but the teacher there "didn't treat Mexicans very well," so they brought their girls here. She seemed disapproving of that attitude toward Mexicans. I saw a lot of Mexicans in Durango and Liberty, and some quiet, oddly-dressed people that Matthew told me were Ute Indians. We live very near their reservation, he said. In fact, the valley Rockytop is in used to be part of the reservation, only recently having been opened up for homesteaders. I'll be teaching the first generation of children— well, white children—to grow up here. Anyway, I found the Archuletas to be very nice people. I certainly won't treat little Teresa and LaQuita any differently than the other students. There's also another little Archuleta girl named Wanda, but she's too young for school and Mrs. Arch—I mean Maria—is expecting this winter. I met another expectant mother, Alice Fredrickson, Hannah's daughter-in-law. She's expecting about a month before Maria and also has a two-year-old girl. I guess I won't be running out of pupils here anytime soon.

Oh, I must quit dilly-dallying and get to work. It's such a luxury to drink coffee and sit in the sun as long as I want, but duty awaits.

Back in the schoolroom, one of the first things Minta did was set up the class roster and post it on the board where she could look at it frequently and memorize names:

Rockytop School 1919-1920

Haley, Angus	7th grade
Haley, Michael	6th grade
Haley, Mary	5th grade
Fredrickson, Gertrude	4th grade
Fredrickson, Gunner	4th grade
Haley, Robert	4th grade
Woods, Florence	4th grade
Archuleta, Teresa	3rd grade
Valori, Paul	3rd grade
Haley, Judith	2nd grade
Woods, Wendell	2nd grade
Archuleta, LaQuita	1st grade
Haley, Dale	1st grade
Valori, Gina	1st grade

She found the Standards for grades one, two, and three and began matching books and materials to them. The three first graders were four, five, and six years old and had never been to school before. At first she didn't want to take little Gina Valori, a frail, small four-year-old. But Claudia took her aside and explained that Gina had to come to school with her big brother, Paul, so their mother could take care of little two-year-old Joseph, who "wasn't right." Apparently he had "fits" or seizures which took all his mother's strength to control, and were scary for little Gina. Gina acted like school would be scary for her, too. Minta was glad her older brother would be there to help with her. He'd seemed very protective of her at the meeting, holding her hand and letting her hide behind his back whenever an adult tried to talk to her.

The second and third graders, except for Wendell, all knew how to read already. Their former teacher had left notes on their progress as well as that of the older students. Minta wasn't going to worry about lessons for forth through seventh grades until closer to September, but she looked through the teacher's notes and found many references to disciplinary problems, especially with the Haley boys and the Fredrickson twins. It sounded like the ferule had been well used last year.

She was in the middle of moving books to what she had designated as the library shelf when she heard a loud commotion outside. She ran to the open window and looked out into the schoolyard. Several deer were running, jumping over the parts of the fence still standing, and going on to leap over the stream below. She was just thinking they seemed to be afraid of something when two dogs—no! coyotes!— appeared. Then they all disappeared in a cloud of dust along the other side of the valley. So this is what it's like on the frontier, she thought. She'd have to write Lulabelle. Minta had tasted her first venison at the school potluck. Apparently the local families supplemented what they raised with wild game.

Minta realized she'd barely thought of Lulabelle, or her parents, since arriving in Colorado. She'd have to write a letter as promised and then find a way to mail it, preferably from somewhere other than Liberty. Her new life had been so all-consuming that she'd almost been able to forget her old life. But she knew it wouldn't be that easy. It would keep coming back to her. Somehow she'd have to learn how to be Minta forever.

A light tap at the door startled her out of her reverie, and she turned to see—what was his name again? Mr. Woods, and something Biblical . . . Luke, Luke Woods standing in the doorway, hat dangling from one hand. She had already noticed the men here were seldom without hats and seemed to feel incomplete without them.

"Yes, may I help you?" she asked.

"More to the point is, may I help you?" he said. "I just dropped my kids off to visit with the younger Haleys for a few minutes and thought I'd see if you needed a hand with moving things or wood or whatever."

Minta took a quick glance at the roster to remind herself that his kids were Florence and Wendell. She recalled Matthew telling her Luke's wife had died in childbirth along with their third child. She was about to send him away when she remembered something she wanted done.

"Well, since you offered, could you, would you . . . unbolt these desks for me?"

"Unbolt them? What for? Aren't they in the right places?"

"Well, I don't know. I mean, I'd like to be able to rearrange them, move them around, you know, when I'm doing reading groups and such. I know most schools have bolted-down desks, but I've been trying to figure out my lesson plans, and it would be so much easier to be able to . . ."

Luke was frowning and shaking his head. "I think I'd have to get the approval of the other school board members first. The instructions for building the school said where to bolt the desks down, and we followed the instructions exactly. Whoever designed these schools must have known what they were doing."

Minta wanted to reply, "Whoever designed this school was probably a man who never taught a day in his life." But she held her tongue and said meekly instead, "Oh, would you? Bring it up with the other board members?"

"Of course. We'll have another meeting the first part of September, but I'll be seeing them before that and can bring it up informally. Is there anything else I can help you with?"

You haven't been very helpful so far, she thought. "No," she said. "I've just finished rearranging the books and there's plenty of wood in the shed. I think everything's all set for my first day."

He looked disappointed. What was it he really wanted? Oh, no! She remembered what Matthew had said about any available men wanting to court her. No one could court her; that was out of the question. She'd have to figure out a way to discourage men like Luke without alienating them.

"Well, I guess I'll go visit with Fred a bit then. I won't ask him about the desks until I've talked to Jens, though. Fred's got some pretty rigid ideas. You got to approach him the right way."

"Yes, thank you. I'll try to remember that."

"And if my kids give you any trouble now, you just let me know."

"Of course. But I'm sure they'll be fine."

"They're pretty good kids, you know. Since their mama passed on, they've had to hoe a pretty hard row. Florence is only nine, but she's already a pretty good little housekeeper, and Wendell tries to help out as much as he can. I'm hoping school—well, you—will make them feel more normal, more like the other kids, instead of the poor kids with no mama."

"I'll certainly try. But Rachel Haley's children don't have a father, so they won't be the only ones with only one parent."

"Oh, Fred more than makes up for his brother being gone. He treats Rachel's kids just like his own. Supports two families. But I don't have anyone like that around to take the place of a mother for my kids." He looked at her intently.

Oh, please, don't look at me as though I could replace your children's mother, Minta thought. She was getting very self-conscious. Why wouldn't he leave?

"You seem uncomfortable," he said. "The part of your contract about not keeping company with men doesn't apply to me since I'm on the school board. So I hope you don't feel I shouldn't be here."

"Of course you can be here. It's your school. And I have no intention of keeping company with *any* men. I came here to teach, and that's all. Now, if you'll excuse me, I need to clean the outhouses."

He didn't offer to help her with that.

CHAPTER SEVEN
Deception

Thursday, August 28, 1919—*I can't believe how busy I've been and how hard teaching is. Oh, it's fun, too. I love it, as I knew I would, but it's so difficult to manage all the different ages, and subjects, and personalities. And now it's almost time to double the number of students and add four more grades. What am I going to do? Already I spend almost every waking minute planning, teaching, grading, cleaning up, trying to keep one step ahead of my pupils.*

I did manage to get a letter off to "Constance" (Lulabelle), so they'll know I'm all right. I heard that Fred was making a trip down to Farmington, New Mexico, to buy some supplies, and I asked him to take my letter and mail it for me. He didn't seem to suspect anything. I'm still nervous that Edmund will try to find me. I hope I have covered my tracks well enough.

Luke Woods continues to take every opportunity to "stop by" to see me. Fortunately, Wendell is doing fine in school and is no trouble, so I don't have to initiate contact with Luke. I think little Gina Valori is adjusting. At first she cried every day, and then she had to sit on my lap every chance she got. But yesterday she went the whole day without either and seems to be finding her place. Sometimes she falls asleep in the afternoon, her little legs curled under her and her head on her desk, and I just let her sleep. Judith Haley and LaQuita Archuleta have become best friends and help each other to the point I've had to separate them for some of the lessons.

Dale Haley is the main problem so far. He's a smart five-year-old, but I don't think he's really ready for school. He can NOT sit still. I've found that letting him work standing up at one of the bigger desks works better than trying to keep him sitting in his place in the small desk. I see why some teachers have been known to tie kids to their desks, not that I would ever do that. I don't know what I'll do with him when the big kids come in and I need those desks for them.

As I suspected, having the desks bolted down is a nuisance. I've been hesitant to ask Luke about it again, because it might mean I'd have to spend more time alone with him. He seems a very nice man. If circumstances were different . . . . Oh, why did I fall for the first man who paid attention to me?

Minta was interrupted by a knock at her door. She rose, expecting to see Honor or another one of the children bringing her eggs or milk, as they often did. Instead, she was face to face with a real live cowboy. She could tell by the hat, the boots, the horse standing outside, and the smell.

"Yes?" she asked nervously, suddenly aware of how alone she was and how far from help if she needed it.

"Sorry to trouble you, ma'am," he said. "But my horse come up lame all of a sudden. I don't want to ride him any more until I figure out what's wrong. Could I tie him up in the shade in the schoolyard while I go ask Paulo Valori if he can look at him? He's got a good hand with the animals."

"Certainly," she said. "Help yourself. You can draw some water from the well for him, too; there's a trough on the other side."

"Silas," he said suddenly.

"Pardon me?"

"Silas Tower, ma'am. Making your acquaintance."

"Oh, yes, how do you do? I'm Minta Mayfield."

"Yep, I know."

"You do?"

"I surely do. You're all anyone's been talking about the past month."

She felt the color rising to her face. "I hope nothing bad has been said, or if it has, that you don't listen to gossip."

"Oh, no, ma'am. Nothing bad. Just there hasn't been a new person in this valley since me, so it's kind of important."

"Are you new, too?"

"Been here a couple years. I'm bunking over in Piñon Hollow with Old Man Rickerts."

"Oh, yes. I met him at the school potluck. I wondered why he came when he didn't have any children."

"You said the magic words: potluck. That's why he came. Since most of the cooking he gets is either his or mine, he's always looking for a good meal. He and me can't cook worth a darn. And folks around here is famous for their potlucks."

She laughed. She was liking this awkward cowboy in spite of herself. She smiled up into his blue-green eyes, noticing the freckles on his pale skin. His eyes pulled away from hers suddenly.

"Well, I'll hoof it on over to Valoris' then," he said, backing away. "Be back as soon as I can."

After he left, Minta wondered if he was one of the men Matthew had warned her would find excuses to have business at Rockytop in order to meet her. He could have just tied his horse up in the shade by the stream and walked to Valoris' without bothering her.

When he returned, Paulo Valori was with him. They looked at and talked about the horse for quite a while. Finally, she took out cups so they could draw drinks of water for themselves. She knew it was hot in the sun.

"Hello, Paulo," she said. "Nice of you to come help."

"Well, we watch out for each other around here," he said. She remembered Honor telling her something like that on her first day and all the times she'd been reminded of it when students brought her milk, eggs, and fresh butter.

"By the way," Paulo said. "Sophie says why don't you come down and ride to church with us tomorrow? I don't know what your church is. The preacher here's a Methodist, and I guess some of the folks is, too. Our family was Catholic in the old country, but there's not a church close enough to go to. Preacher says God don't care where we go, long as we go. Maybe someday there will be enough of us Catholics to have our own church. Now there's just us and Archuletas, but they won't go to a Protestant Church. When they can, they go into Liberty. Most everyone else that's anything is some kind of Protestant."

"Thank you, I'd love to go. Methodist is fine." In fact, it was more than fine. It was the church she'd been raised in. Edmund had insisted she go to his church, Lutheran. It wasn't that different in doctrine from Methodist, but she had missed the homey feel of her old church. She agreed with the preacher about God not caring which. It was your intentions that counted. And whether you were right with God. That was something Minta had been having trouble with. It was hard to feel right with God when she was deceiving His people. Maybe getting back to going to church would help.

The two men decided the horse had probably stepped on a rock wrong and bruised its foot. They wrapped it in a cleaning rag she gave them, and Silas started the long walk home, leading the horse so that he wouldn't do any more damage to the injury with his weight.

"You know Silas loves that horse," Paulo said as they walked off.

"Why do you say that?"

"Because he's willing to walk all that way home. There's nothing a cowboy hates worse than walking. I think it's because they wear such uncomfortable boots."

"He said he lives with Mr. Rickerts. Are they related?"

"No. Rickerts hired him a couple summers ago to help move cattle, and he just stayed. I think he was a drifter. He'll probably up and drift off again somewheres else one of these days. Well, I'd better get on home. See you bright and early tomorrow."

"I'll be there."

Minta was up early and ready for church in her best outfit an hour before time to leave. The embroidered white blouse and black skirt accented her small waist. She brushed her hair until it was a mass of flyaway static. She couldn't get used to how dry it was here. Her hair and skin were so dry all the time. The Archuleta girls had brought her some pitch salve that their mother made from the sap of the piñon trees. She rubbed it into her hands and elbows several times a day, and it helped. She didn't know what to do about her hair, though. Finally she was able to twist it into a knot and secure it with pins so that her good black hat would fit over it. She was so happy to be going to church without worrying about being late or having to leave early. She could even visit with people afterwards!

The church was several miles downstream near where Halpern Creek emptied into the Liberty River, across from the Halpern School, which looked just like Rockytop and Shady Rest. Most of the people she'd already met were there, as well as many she didn't know—people from Piñon Hollow and the Halpern area. She sat next to Sophia and let Gina climb onto her lap, leaving Sophie's free for Joseph. Paul sat between his parents. The wooden benches were smooth but uncomfortable. She sat up straight, her backbone bumping painfully against the bench back whenever Gina squirmed. When Minta had fidgeted in church and complained about being uncomfortable, her grandmother always told her she didn't have enough "padding." It was still true, although she had begun to gain back some of the weight she'd lost at Edmund's. Just the other day, she had to let her skirt out another tuck.

The minister started with a few announcements and prayer concerns, then pointed at the empty piano bench and said, "As you can see, Mrs. Carpenter isn't here today. We need to pray for her quick recovery. So we'll just have to sing without accompaniment this morning. For our first song, let's turn to . . ."

Honor stood up and pointed at Minta. "Reverend MacIntosch? Miss Mayfield can play the piano."

Minta realized everyone had suddenly turned to look at her. She felt her face going hot.

"Is that true, Miss . . . Mayfield, was it? Would you do us the honor of playing for us?" Reverend MacIntosch asked.

"Well, I haven't practiced," she stammered. "I don't know which ones you . . ."

"Oh, that's all right. You pick the songs. We'll just do what you know today."

And that's what they did. She sat at the piano in front and turned to songs she knew in the hymnal. She started with "The Old Rugged Cross." It was relatively easy to play and was the first song she'd ever played publicly in her childhood church when she was thirteen and it had just been published. Her piano teacher loved getting the most up-to-date songs. It seemed fitting to start with it here. The songs in the hymnal were mostly familiar to her from when she played regularly at her church throughout her teen years. Once she got over her nervousness, she actually enjoyed herself. And she found the piano bench much more comfortable than the other seats.

After church, the congregation showed no signs of hurrying home. They all wanted to stay and talk to each other. She got many compliments on her playing, the best one from Honor, who said, "You play much better than Mrs. Carpenter. She pounds on the keys like she's trying to beat the piano to death, and she doesn't keep a steady rhythm; then she gets mad at us if we don't keep up with her. I wish you could do it all the time."

Minta was disappointed she didn't get to meet Claire Carpenter. She was the widow who taught at Piñon Hollow, and she wanted to ask her how she handled so many different grades and subjects.

She did meet Ben Griffith, his wife, who appeared to be with child, and their two little boys. He was the Halpern teacher. But in spite of his small stature, coming only up to her shoulder, he seemed so arrogant and self-confident that she didn't feel comfortable asking him for advice. He told her that a young woman had just been hired for Shady Rest School, but she wouldn't be there for two more weeks.

"So, they'll be getting a late start," he said. "I heard you've already begun. I start tomorrow."

"I've only begun with the primaries. The secondaries start coming tomorrow," she replied. "I'm a little nervous about that," she admitted.

"Don't let them get the best of you," he said. "Use the ferule the first day. That's what I do. Then they'll know you're serious, and the rest of the year will go more smoothly."

"Yes, I'm sure it will," she replied, edging away from him, reminded of the seriousness of her job starting tomorrow. The little ones were easy to control without corporal punishment, but she was worried about the older ones whose reputations preceded them. "I must see where the Valoris are. I don't want to miss my ride back."

"And start your group practicing softball," he called to her as she walked away. "Halpern is still undefeated, but we'd like some real competition in the tournament this year." His laughter followed her. She'd have to find out what all that was about. She supposed the older kids would know.

All the way back she worried about her first "real" day of teaching, Ben Griffith's words haunting her. She'd find another way to show them she was serious—like good teaching, for example.

The first day with all fourteen students turned out to be both better and worse than she expected. It was better in that most of them were on their best behavior, excited about being back in school—the "Honeymoon Period," as her professor at Normal called the first week of school. After that they would test her.

It was worse in that the added grades, ages, and bodies made for even more confusion than she'd counted on. She had made a seating chart and made them all sit there to start with. She had to double up some of the younger ones in desks, since there were only twelve for fourteen students. But, already, she could tell she wouldn't be able to sit them with their age and grade all the time. Gertie and Gunny had to be separated, as did Angus and Michael. In fact, Angus couldn't sit near any of the younger boys, who all looked up to him and took their cues from him. She didn't need him leading them astray with his anti-school attitude. And Dale was squirming in his small seat all day, used to being able to stand at one of the bigger ones. Somehow, someway, she was

going to get these seats unbolted and arrange the room for *her* conven-
ience, not some architect's. She had already tried to do it herself and
determined she wasn't strong enough to loosen the bolts.

She could tell her biggest challenge would be the "fours," as she
called them. The four fourth graders: Gertie, Gunny, Robert, and
Florence. The only one who seemed to know how to sit still and pay
attention was Florence. And she couldn't put Florence in-between all
three of the others.

Well, it was only the first day. They'd all settle down. She hoped.

❖ ❖ ❖

The first week passed so quickly that she was surprised to wake up
one morning and realize it was Saturday. That was the day she had
decided to scrub the school floors, so after her usual oatmeal and coffee breakfast, she carried her bucket and scrub brush to the school.
Edmund hated oatmeal. The one time she'd fixed it for his breakfast,
he'd yelled, "You don't expect me to eat this pig swill?" and flung it
against the wall, breaking one of her wedding bowls and leaving a mess
for her to clean up. He'd stomped out of the house shouting, "I'm
going to do the chores. When I get back, there had better be a proper
breakfast on this table!" Now she could have oatmeal every day if she
wished, and she usually did.

She was on her knees, scrubbing the schoolroom floor, her ging-
ham work dress bunched up around her hips when she heard a scuffle
of boots in the cloakroom behind her. She rose quickly, brushing down
the skirt and pushing out of her eyes a wing of hair that had escaped
the pins.

Luke was standing, hat in hand, as he'd done the first day he came.
"Morning, Minta," he said.

"I hope you've come to tell me you can help unbolt these desks
now. I know you had a meeting last night."

"Yes, we did. And I voted to unbolt them, really I did, Minta,
but . . ."

"But?"

"Well, you know how Fred is. He's kind of set in his ways. He said bolted-down desks worked fine when he was in school, so they'd work fine for his passel of kids, too. I thought Jens might go along with me but, well, Fred's a hard man to cross, if you know what I mean."

"So Jens voted with Fred," she finished for him.

"Sorry, Minta. I don't see what difference it makes, as long as the kids learn."

"Exactly. What difference could it possibly make to Fred?" she said, her eyes narrowing. She'd like to see Fred try to control fourteen kids in the confines of the twelve unmovable desks. But then, if Fred were the teacher, they'd be afraid to move.

"I'm sorry to have to be the one to bring you the news, Minta. But I was wondering if maybe you'd join me and my two for supper tonight anyway? I've gotten pretty good at cooking since Martha . . . passed on . . . and Florence, she's a good little baker. She's home now, making you a cake."

Minta racked her brain for a way to escape; but dragging the children into it made her hesitant to refuse. She'd been invited to meals at several of the other students' homes and had gone. How could she refuse Luke just because she thought he had ulterior motives?

"All right," she finally said. "But I can't stay long. I find it takes all my free time just to stay one step ahead of these kids and their lessons."

He smiled. "I'll bet it does."

"By the way, how was the motion, or whatever it was, to unbolt the desks worded?" she asked.

"I just said, 'I make a motion we unbolt the desks like she wants.' Why?"

"I just wondered," she said, her mind already working. So they had voted that "they" would not unbolt the desks. They didn't vote that the desks could not be unbolted. She knew it was a thin straw, but she'd grasp at anything at this point. She was good at making and carrying out plans on her own; she'd learned that escaping from Edmund. She'd put those skills to work and get the desks the way she wanted them.

Luke's words came back to her, "Fred's a hard man to cross." Was she sure she wanted to cross Fred already? Well, if the opportunity presented itself, she would.

Opportunity, in the form of Silas Tower, presented itself that afternoon. He stopped to water his horse at the school trough, and she took out a biscuit spread with Claudia's fresh butter and jam, left over from her lunch, and offered it to him.

"Thank you," he said. "I already ate some jerky I packed along, but this tastes right good. Rickerts' biscuits look like little dried up cow pies, taste like 'em, too, and mine are worse."

She laughed at the image of cow-pie biscuits. "Do you have time to help me with something at the school?" she asked.

After showing him what she had in mind, he said, "It'll take a tool I don't have. Maybe I could borrow one from Fred."

"No, don't do that. Paulo's place is a little closer. Maybe he has one."

"Okay, I'll ride over and see."

"Thanks, and, if you don't have to, don't tell him what you need it for, okay?"

"Planning a little surprise are you?"

"Something like that."

He returned with the tool and spent the better part of an hour unbolting most of the desks. The last one was proving to be particularly stubborn.

"I just can't loosen this last bolt, Minta," he said. "I need more muscle. Do you want me to go see if Paulo will come help?"

"No, let me try to help you first. Maybe the two of us together can get it."

"Okay. Sit here in front of me and grab on here. When I say three, lean back and give her all the muscle you got. Okay? One . . . two . . . three!" They both leaned back and pulled as hard as they could. Suddenly, the bolt came loose and threw them back together, Minta on top of Silas, in a heap on the floor. He was laughing, his arms around her, as she struggled to get up. She finally managed it, and they both stood, backing away from each other, their faces identical shades of hot pink, suddenly shy.

Silas found his voice first. "Now what?" he asked. "They're loose, where do you want them?"

"I don't know."

"You don't know! Slitherin' snakes, what did we just do all this for then?"

"I mean, I want to try them in different arrangements. Slide them all over by the windows so I can sweep where they were. Then I'll tell you where to put them. Or I can do it, now that they're loose. I don't mean to take up your whole afternoon."

"That's all right. I was just going to ride into town for something to do. But I don't really have any important business there. Hey, why don't you come with me? We could get some supper at the hotel. It's a full moon tonight, and . . . ." He stopped when he saw the dismay on her face.

"I'm sorry, Silas. I'm already invited to supper tonight. With the family of some of my students," she added hastily, so he wouldn't think she had a date with another man.

"Maybe another time, then," Silas said.

Minta was silent. What was she doing leading Silas on like this? What would he think if he knew she was married and had lied about her name? What would any of them think? Why was this all so much harder than she'd thought it would be when her main concern had been escaping Edmund? She knew what her grandmother would say: "Oh, what a tangled web we weave when first we practice to deceive."

CHAPTER EIGHT

Confrontation

ༀ

Saturday, September 20, 1919—*How time flies when you're having fun, as my grandmother used to say. And I am having fun. Except for a few times like having to suffer through dinner at the Woods' with the kids too eager to please me and their father worse. Enough said about that. I'll just have to figure out a graceful way to decline future invitations from Luke Woods.*

I've figured out a daily schedule that seems to be working. The students do better when things are ordered and predictable, so I try to stick to my schedule. I know it's dangerous to brag too soon. My words will come back to haunt me if it all falls apart. But, so far, so good. I've found a discipline plan that is working, too. I used the children's interest in softball and made a "Three Strikes and You're Out" rule. Strike One, the offender's name goes on the board. Strike Two, an X goes behind his or her name. Strike Three, punishment occurs. That's usually banishment to the chair I put in the cloakroom for that purpose. They hate to be separated from each other and the activity of the classroom, so they aren't anxious to repeat a stay there. So far, anyway.

Last Sunday afternoon Honor and Mary came to my door with a basket. I lifted the cloth expecting more eggs and found two kittens. The girls said I needed them for mouse control, and I guess I do. I've seen some evidence of mouse activity behind the stove and in the dugout I use for storage. Mother never allowed cats or dogs in the house, nor did Edmund. But the girls warned me not to leave the kittens outside at night because of the coyotes and owls and other predators that would get them. I didn't have the heart to lock them in the woodshed, so they've become my companions. I named the mostly black one "Blackie"; she's a female. The girls wanted me to name the gray striped one "Smokey" because it looks like he has smoke rings around him. It's so much fun to watch them play together. I'm afraid I'm getting very attached.

So far I haven't experienced any repercussions from unbolting the desks. I'm sure the children have chattered about it at home, so their parents must know. I know the kids tell me everything that goes on at home, probably greatly exaggerated, so I'm sure they do the same at home about school. But if anyone (Fred) objects, I'm ready for him. I think.

At 7 a.m. Minta carried in the two water buckets for the day's drinking water and hand washing. Then she began writing the day's lessons on the boards. She needed all three boards for all the different subjects and grades. The pupils kept up with their work better if they had the instructions written in front of them all day. Then she graded papers until time to ring the first bell at 8:15, which told them they had fifteen minutes to get ready to come inside. At 8:30 she rang the final bell and they lined up by age, youngest first, to come in.

Then they stood by their seats for "morning exercises," which weren't really exercises but all the beginning routines of the school day. They always started with the pledge to the flag, followed by Minta playing one or more of several patriotic songs she was teaching them to sing. Then they could sit down and Minta would take roll and read to them for about ten minutes from whichever book they were currently reading. Right now it was *The Wind in the Willows*. The students never wanted to be late and miss what was happening next. The older boys rolled their eyes and pretended not to be interested, but she could tell they were caught up in the story, too.

By nine she began the schedule of classes which lasted throughout most of the day. First were the reading classes for the primaries while the secondaries did geography and history. The older students worked by themselves according to the directions on the board while she listened to the little ones read. After they had all read, she gave them seat work to do while she orally quizzed the older ones on their lessons. If an older student did especially well or finished work early, he or she was allowed to help one or more of the younger students, a coveted job.

At 10:15 everyone got a fifteen-minute recess. Sometimes Minta went out with them, but more often she had to catch up with grading their work or get ready for the next session. When she couldn't go out, she tried to keep an eye and ear on the windows to make sure all was going well. Mary was good about watching out for the younger kids, but the big boys sometimes got into trouble if they thought she wasn't looking. In fact, on one of her trips to the windows, she caught Robert climbing the lone, scraggly pine tree in the schoolyard, which was against the rules, not so much because it was dangerous, but because it was too hard on the tree. She warned him that she had put his name on the board.

At 10:30 she rang the bell and they lined up to come back in. They'd just started the post-recess math session when Fred came in and stood awkwardly in the back of the classroom. Minta looked up and said, "Yes, Fred, may I help you?"

He strode to the front of the room to meet her at her desk which she deliberately hadn't vacated, feeling it gave her some status or power. As he passed by the first graders, he stopped and asked, "Dale, why aren't you sitting in your seat like everyone else?"

Minta got up and went and stood by Dale, putting her hand on his shoulder reassuringly. "Dale," she said, "go sit in that desk for a minute, I want to show your father something." Dale obediently sat in one of the small desks next to Judy as directed. "Look here, Fred," Minta said. "This is the smallest desk we have, and his feet don't even reach the floor. It's very uncomfortable for him to sit like that for very long. His toes go to sleep and he says he gets all 'pwickly' inside his feet and has to squirm around. So I allow him to work standing up part of the time, or even sitting on the floor. There aren't enough desks for everyone anyway. Go back to your work now, Dale." He returned to his position standing at the taller desk opposite Gunny while Fred frowned.

"Actually, it was about the desks that I came," he said. "Didn't Luke tell you we decided that they couldn't be unbolted?"

"Let's discuss it in the cloakroom," she said, drawing him back with her and shutting the door behind them, all too aware of the fourteen pair of ears that had perked up to listen to them.

"No, Luke didn't tell me the desks couldn't be unbolted," she said. "He told me that you all voted that *you* would not unbolt the desks. He didn't say you voted that it couldn't be done."

Fred frowned. "It's that kind of manipulative shenanigans that would earn my kids a trip to the woodshed," he said.

"Well, I'm not one of your kids. I'm an adult, and I was hired to teach this school the best way I know how. And in my *professional* judgment, having the desks unbolted is in the students' best interest."

"But why? I don't see what difference it makes, except it looks disorderly."

"Come back into the classroom and I'll show you," she said.

They reentered to one of the most orderly classrooms she'd ever seen. Everyone was working like his or her life depended on it.

"Look at the holes where the desks were bolted," she said. "See how close together they were? It's very hard for kids to sit still, pay attention, and do their work when they're right on top of each other like that. Now, see how I have it now? The fourth grade has its own section over there. The older kids who are just one to a grade can be moved away from the center of the room to individual spots, so they aren't bothered by the younger kids reading aloud. If I find an arrangement isn't working, I can change it. And best of all, when winter comes, I'll be able to move all the desks out of the way so students can have recess inside and still play some games that take space."

Fred didn't seem to have an answer as he looked around the room. Finally he said, "And what about the chair I saw out in the cloakroom? What's that all about?"

"That's part of my discipline plan."

"Is that this 'Three Strikes and You're Dead' thing the kids have been talking about?"

She smiled at their exaggeration. "Three Strikes and You're Out," she corrected. "When someone breaks a rule or is disruptive or disobeys, I put his name on the board and then . . ." She realized her mistake as soon as she gestured to the board and Fred turned to see "Robert " written there. Robert slid down in his seat as far as he could, his red neck showing above the back of the seat and his face buried in his book as Fred turned to glower at him.

"Come back to the cloakroom, Fred," Minta said quickly. "There's something else I want to discuss with you."

"Well?" he said when they were back with the door closed.

"As I was saying about *my* discipline plan, when they reach three strikes, punishment occurs. Robert only has one. I'm sure he'll be fine the rest of the day. That's usually how it works. They seldom get past one or two strikes."

"That's silly, giving them three chances. You should paddle them the first time they do something wrong. Why all this dilly-dallying around?"

"Because, Fred, they're here to learn. And one way they learn is from their mistakes. When they see their names on the board, it reminds them of what they did and not to do it again. It also reminds the other students of proper behavior. And it gives them some control over their own behavior. They have to *choose* to be good, which is what we want them to do in the long run, isn't it?"

He didn't answer, frowning as he thought about it.

She finally said, "I appreciate your interest in the school, Fred. Of course, you are welcome to come in any time, as is your right as a board member. But when you do, I have to ask that you just observe and not interfere with what I'm doing with the students."

"But my job as the school board president is to make sure everything's going right down here. To make sure you're doing your job."

"*Your* job, as I see it, Fred, is to oversee the general workings of the school. Making sure I'm meeting the terms of my contract. Handling complaints parents have. Like if kids are coming home from school crying and saying they hate school, then I would expect you to step in and see what's going on. But it's not *your* job to do *my* job, the everyday details of running the classroom. That's what you hired me to do. Now will you let me go back in there and do that?"

A vein in Fred's neck throbbed as if he were holding back his anger. Finally he said, "All right, Minta. For now. But if I do get complaints from other parents, I'll be back."

"I'm sure you will," she said quietly to his retreating back. Then she took a deep breath and reentered the classroom.

"Is he gone?" Angus asked, looking up from his math paper.

"Yes."

She could feel as well as hear the sigh of relief that flooded the room from everyone except Robert.

"Thanks a lot, Miss Mayfield! Why did you have to go and write my name on the board just before my father came?" Robert whined.

"Excuse me, Robert," she whirled around and stomped to his desk, looking down from her considerable height at him, hands on her hips, "Whose fault is it that your name is on the board?"

He squirmed in his seat but finally answered, "Mine, ma'am."

She turned to the rest of the class. "That's right. And don't any of you forget it," she said, shaking her left index finger at them. "Any of your parents can come in here any time. If you don't want them to see your names on the board, it's up to you to behave in such a manner that that doesn't happen. Is that clear?"

"Jeeze Louise," Gertie said. "You don't have to yell at all of us with your teacher voice and get out your teacher finger."

Several students started to laugh. Minta walked to the board and wrote under Robert's name, "Gertie." The room returned to silence.

After lunch recess, Minta always did grammar. She had found that grammar, as well as math—which she did right before lunch—were the weakest subjects overall for most of them. It seemed last year's teacher had just let them move ahead with both subjects, even if they hadn't mastered the previous lesson. So most were hopelessly behind and lost. Minta made sure they understood each concept before they were allowed to go on to the next. That meant she was teaching the same thing to some of the older students as to the third and fourth graders. It also provided a big incentive for the older ones to improve, because they didn't like to be stuck with the younger classes.

Mary, with her quick mind and dedication to her studies, had rapidly improved and was back to grade level in both subjects. Angus had improved in math but was still hopelessly lost in grammar, and hated it, besides. Michael went along with Angus, even though she suspected he could do the work on his own if he tried. She was despairing about what to do with them when help arrived in the form of Honor.

"Now that most of the fall garden work is done," Honor said, "Mother says I can come help every Wednesday if you'd still like me to."

"Oh, Honor, I'd love to have your help. But I can't pay you, you know."

"I know. I thought maybe . . . I was hoping . . . would you give me piano lessons in exchange?"

So it was arranged. Minta had Honor work with individual students on Wednesdays, getting them caught up with whatever they had missed or not understood. Her verbal good nature appealed to the kids, and they worked well with her, even her siblings. After school on Wednesdays, Minta gave Honor piano lessons. Honor walked or rode her horse over whenever she could before or after school and on weekends to practice. The school was always unlocked. She took to reading music quickly and was fast becoming a competent player.

Minta decided to have Honor play a piece at the Christmas program, even though she was out of school. The kids had told her the first week of school that they needed to start planning the Christmas program.

"So soon?" Minta asked. "Why the rush?"

"We have to do so much to get ready. We should be practicing every Friday and learning our pieces by heart," Mary said.

"What do you usually do?" Minta asked.

"Last year we each had a poem we had to memorize and say, and the older kids had to say a prose piece, too, like a famous speech or something," Mary answered over the groans of the boys.

"And we always sing Christmas songs. That will be so much better this year since you can really play the piano," Mary continued, ignoring them.

"Who comes to this?" Minta asked.

"Oh, everyone—all the families and even some that don't have kids in school, and Mr. and Mrs. Post come from town if the roads aren't too bad with snow or mud," Mary answered.

"And you have to invite Santa Claus. He has to come, too," Wendell said.

"Santa Claus? But how . . ."

"Shh," Mary said, her eyes sparkling. "I'll tell you later."

Mary lingered after the others went out to afternoon recess. "Mr. Rickerts is Santa, Miss Mayfield. You just send word to him when the program is, and he'll be here. He has the suit and everything. But don't tell the little ones, you know. They still believe in the real Santa."

Angus was still in the room, too, waiting to talk to Minta. "I ain't saying no memory piece this year," he said.

Minta frowned. "Say that again, grammatically correctly."

"Okay. But I'm not going to do any memory piece."

"Why not? You have a perfectly good memory. You told us the scores of every softball game Rockytop played for the last five years just the other day."

"I can't be up in front of people like that. Adults, I mean. If you make me, I'll . . . I'll run away from school and never come back." He folded his arms and set his chin in the gesture she knew meant there would be no budging him without a major fight.

"I'm sure we can figure out something you can do for the program, Angus."

"I doubt it," he said, stomping out of the room. "I don't see why we have to have a gol-durned Christmas program anyway."

The next Wednesday she asked Honor about the Christmas program after they finished the piano lesson. Honor told about all the ones she remembered being in and which ones were best and why. They all sounded pretty similar, with songs, readings from the Bible, memory pieces, and then refreshments. Santa arrived while refreshments were being eaten and passed out bags of goodies to each child.

"The school board really comes up with the bags of stuff," Honor said. "They hide them in your cabin and Santa picks them up there on his way in."

"I see," Minta said. "So it's a pretty important night to everyone, isn't it?'

"Oh, yes. I heard Father telling Mother that the Christmas program was one of the most important parts of the school year because it was the first time the community really got a good look at how the teacher is doing. One year, after the Christmas program, the teacher never came back. We only had half a year of school that year."

Minta was beginning to agree with Angus about not wanting to participate in the program. "Honor, do you know why Angus is so dead set against being in the program?"

"Well, last year he had a memory piece. He had it all learned. He even recited it to me on the way to and from school every day the last week before the program, so I know he knew it by heart. But then the night of the program, when it was his turn, he just turned red and couldn't get more than the first few words out. He ran out the door and went home. Didn't even stay for Santa. Then when we got home; Father gave him a whipping for leaving like that and for not knowing his piece. But he really did know it. I'm sure of that."

"I see," Minta said.

Chapter Nine

Disasters

ৎ৵৶৻

Friday, September 26, 1919—*Well, I've figured out the Christmas program. I don't want to do the same thing every other teacher has done. I want it to be unique. Finally, I got the idea to write a play. Once I decided what to write about, it went pretty fast. I worked on it mornings before school, getting up an hour earlier than usual to have more time. I know how many kids I have to work with and what they'll be able to handle, so I wrote it around that. I also need to do something that we don't need expensive or difficult costumes or props for. I decided to make it set in "the Old West," so they can wear their regular clothes and use things they have at home for props.*

We've started rehearsals. I only let them practice Friday afternoons, if they get their morning work done, and they are doing very well with that. We decided to keep the play a secret from their parents. When anyone asks what they're doing for the program, they decided to say, "We're memorizing something and singing some songs." Both of those are true; they have to memorize their parts and sing some songs during the play.

I wanted Angus and Mary to have the leads, as they're the oldest boy and girl, but Angus would have none of it, of course, so Michael has the role of Joseph. I'm still trying to figure out what Angus can do. I'm determined he participate somehow as I know Fred will be upset if he doesn't.

Oops. Smokey just ran across the table and caused me to smear the ink. Those two are growing so fast. I hope they soon learn to channel some of their energy into catching mice instead of each other. They stalk each other all over the cabin, hiding behind table legs, then jumping out, backs arched, tails up, bouncing sideways at each other until one of them starts chasing the other. Then they're tearing all over, up across the bed, over the table, behind the stove, around and around. I do enjoy watching them, though. The kittens and the children are what bring joy into my life these days.

How did I get so lucky to have landed in this place with these people? Everyone is so good to me—even Fred, although he's a pain to deal with. I feel guilty every time I think of the deception I've perpetrated on them all. I try to teach their children to have good moral values and tell the truth, and what am I? A runaway bride and a liar. I pray and pray but so far I've gotten no relief from these feelings. The only time it leaves me is when I immerse myself in my job and forget everything except my day-to-day duties. Sometimes I wish there were someone I could confide in. But I don't dare, not even to Rev. MacIntosch. The thought of being forced to leave here is even worse than dealing with my guilty conscience. At least it makes me a little more understanding toward my students when they lie to save their skin or seem to have something on their consciences.

Angus and Michael had been out all week helping with the gathering and moving of cattle. Minta prepared lessons for Mary to take home, so Honor could help the boys catch up on their schoolwork. Minta hadn't understood at first when they tried to tell her about what they'd be doing. "But where are the cattle? Don't you keep them on your farm?" she asked when Mary told her the two boys would be absent all week.

"Not in the summer," Mary explained. "In the summer they go up to the higher mountains where there's better pasture and more water. Then in the fall, before the heavy snows, we bring them back down."

"But, do you just leave them there all alone? Who takes care of them?"

"Where they are has lots of grass and water, and they're fenced in so they can't wander too far off. But it's a big area—they get spread out, and sometimes it's hard to find them all to bring them back. That's why it takes most of the week for the gathering. And Silas goes up once a week to check on them and the fences, and sometimes the other men do, too. All the Rockytop cattle are together. It's only a day's ride up and back."

"Then why does it take so long to bring them back?"

"A day's ride on a horse is a lot faster than trying to drive a whole herd of cattle. It takes several days to do that. You have to let them stop and graze and rest sometimes. And gather up all the ones that wander off."

Sometimes Minta thought she was learning more than the kids were. She'd had a lesson in grubbing sagebrush her first week there. It grew wild everywhere there weren't trees and had to be cut down, and then the roots had to be hacked out of the ground to make pastures and fields. It was backbreaking work, much of it done by the kids.

The week without the two older boys was almost over, and Minta had to admit it had been nice teaching without the frequent high jinks and challenges to her authority that Michael and, especially, Angus perpetrated. On Wednesday she and Honor had taken the students on a walk to look at trees. Their old, handed-down *Natural School Geography* book, published in 1898, only had a short paragraph on the forests of the Rocky Mountains. It read, *The forests are confined to the mountain slopes, which they sometimes cover to the height of 10,000 to 12,000 feet. The timber has been greatly reduced by forest fires, and by the demands of railway building and mining, and the like. The trees are mostly pines, firs, cedars, hemlocks, spruces, and other conifers.*

"Who knows the altitude here?" she asked.

Robert raised his hand. "There's a sign at Liberty that says it's 8,050 feet, and it's uphill from us, so we're a little lower than that, I guess."

"What kinds of trees do we have here?" she asked.

"Green," LaQuita volunteered.

"Piney ones," Wendell offered.

"Vehwy big ones," Dale said.

So they went for a walk to look at trees—first the cottonwoods and willows by the river and then the pines on the higher ground so they could see the differences between deciduous trees and conifers.

Minta was on new ground in more ways than one when they got into the pine forest. From a distance all the trees looked the same, but when she got among them she could see two different kinds. Fortunately Honor came to her rescue and explained to the younger kids which were the piñons and which the junipers, or "cedars," as most people called them.

Minta paid attention, noticing for the first time the differences in the needles—long and spiky on the piñon and shorter and softer on the juniper. The juniper also had little blue-green berries, which weren't really berries but seeds. The juniper bark was gray and pieces of it shed off in long peels, while the piñon's bark was brown and more like the tree bark she was used to.

They found a piñon that had been damaged by a porcupine chewing on the bark, and sticky sap, or pitch, oozed out of the wound which nearly circled the tree. Teresa tried to explain how her mother made pitch salve, but it was too complicated. Several of the boys broke off pieces of the gooey substance and chewed it like gum. Minta declined a sample. She said she thought she liked the junipers best because of their bluish color and graceful branches.

"If you're in the woods during a thunderstorm, stay away from the junipers," Robert said.

"You should stay away from all trees in a thunderstorm," Minta said.

"Yeah, but, if you're in the woods and all there is is trees, stay by the piñons."

"Why is that?"

"'Cause if lightning is going to strike, it will always strike a juniper and not a piñon. My father says he's seen it time and time again." The other kids nodded their agreement.

Before they went back to the classroom, Minta had the kids each break a piece off of a tree. Then they had a writing assignment in which they had to try to describe the smell of whatever tree they picked. The best description was by Florence, who wrote, "When I close my eyes and smell my piece of piñon, my nose tells me it's Christmas."

On Friday, Dale came running in from afternoon recess shouting, "They'a coming; they'a coming!"

"Who's coming?" Minta asked.

"The cattle. We can see the dust, and you can heah them, too. Come look!"

Minta went outside to where the kids were all leaning against the parts of the north fence that were still standing. She could see the cloud of dust approaching and hear the distant cries of the cattle. The dust reminded her of how long it had been since she'd seen rain—not since before school started, and that was just a brief shower. There was a feeling in the air that made her nervous.

"Let's go in," she said. "Recess should have been over several minutes ago."

"Can't we stay out and watch?" Gunner begged. "I'm going on the drive next year."

"No you aren't," Gertie responded. "You know you can't go until you're twelve."

Minta made them reenter the classroom, but as the herd got closer and closer, she realized there would be no more teaching occurring that afternoon. At least by her. Even play practice held no interest for them in light of the more exciting activities going on outside, and there wasn't much point in practicing without Michael.

She let the students line up at the windows to watch the herd go by and was immediately glad she hadn't given in to their pleas to stay outside. The broken-down fence was no match for the stragglers that left the road and wandered across the schoolyard leaving large fresh pies to go with the dried up ones she'd been battling all fall. Some of the cattle were running, and all of them were much, much bigger than her students. Little Gina could have been trampled in a instant, or anyone else, for that matter.

The older boys had invented a game they called Cow Pie Bull's Eye. They set up a target on a fence post and then drew lines in the dirt for each age of boy, the oldest farthest back. They had to stand behind their line and try to hit the bull's eye with a dried-up cow patty. They got points based on where it hit the target and if it broke apart on impact.

At first, disgusted by their picking up the things, she had thought about making a rule against the game. Then she decided more rules just meant more breaking of rules and more punishments she had to mete out. In the end, she settled for insisting that they wash their hands when they came in. They didn't seem to mind that, especially since it meant a few more minutes before they had to return to their seats.

Now she realized why the schoolyard had yielded such a large number of pieces of ammunition for their game. The fence offered no deterrent to a cow who wanted to come in.

Silas had passed by with the first bunch of cattle. Then a long stream of cows rumbled by before any other riders came into sight. From a distance, Michael and Angus looked tired and dusty, slumped in their saddles, barely holding on to the reins. As they came into line with the school, though, they sat up tall in their saddles and began shouting instructions to the cattle, making sure all the kids saw the importance of their jobs and their contribution to the cattle drive.

Michael rode up next to a cow trying to go down to the stream. "Hi, ha! You ornery skunk. Git along now," he yelled, using the pressure of his knees to signal the horse as he flicked his rope against the cow's hide. The cow seemed to respond—more to the horse than to Michael.

After the last cows had battered their way through the schoolyard, Dale pointed to the corner where the younger children played and shouted, "Aw, shucks. They wuined ouwa fahms. Evwething's all gone."

Minta had gone out one recess a few weeks ago to see what the younger kids were doing so intently in the corner of the schoolyard that they had staked out for themselves. She found them busily making farms and ranches by scratching out fence lines, roads, and ditches with sticks. They had different rocks for different things: the whitish-gray pebbles were sheep, the brownish-black ones were horses and cattle. Especially interesting rocks were people, and sometimes dogs.

They were chattering happily, intent on their game, when she walked up to them; but when she started questioning them about their activities, they got strangely quiet. Finally Dale said, "We don't want to talk about it, Miss, we just want to do it." She took the hint and left them to their labors. They spent nearly every recess refining their farms and ranches and moving livestock rocks from one place to another. Now, after seeing how the cattle had to be moved, she understood why.

Looking at the hoof prints and cow pies where their farms had been, Dale seemed on the verge of tears. Robert knelt down beside him. "It's all right, Dale. You'll just have to start all over, like real farmers do when something bad happens."

"Yeah," Dale said. "We could pwetend a dwought came and the gwasshoppas et evwething up."

"And then there was a big forest fire that burned up all the buildings and trees," Wendell added.

"And then the floods came and washed everything out," Paul said.

"My goodness, you kids know a lot of disasters," Minta exclaimed.

Robert gave her a funny look. "It's all stuff that happens here, Teacher," he said.

As if to punctuate Robert's statement, a bolt of lightning lit up the sky with thunder following quickly. They had been so intent on watching the herd arriving from the north, they hadn't seen the storm clouds approaching from the southwest.

"Get your things together quickly," Minta ordered. "We'll let out a few minutes early today. Maybe you can make it home before the rain."

They left in a cluster of excitement over the rain and the cattle. Minta was learning that what were everyday occurrences elsewhere were often the cause of great excitement here. Not that rain was an everyday occurrence. A brief shower the day before school started did no more than leave brown spots on the windows which had to be washed off. It hadn't even settled the dust. No wonder the water in the stream was down to a barely noticeable trickle and people were worriedly checking their wells every day. Fred had come and checked the school well. It was still all right.

"What do we do if it goes dry?" she asked.

"Then we start hauling water from the spring over on Rickerts' place. Hope it don't come to that. September is usually our rainiest month."

The first drops were falling when Minta dashed from the school to her cabin. The half-grown kittens followed her in, shaking their fur indignantly at the unaccustomed drops of moisture. Inside, they each immediately began licking themselves, getting rid of the disgusting water. She had to laugh at them. They usually came over to the school-yard each recess and let the children pet them. They rebelled at being carried around too much, though, and she'd had to doctor several scratches on the younger kids who didn't take the cats' squirming to get down seriously enough.

There was a hole in the bottom left corner of her cabin door. At first, she'd planned to ask the school board to fix it for her, but it had become the way the cats got in and out at will. It was much easier than having to get up all the time to open the door, and if she wanted them to stay in or out, all she had to do was set her carpetbag in front of the opening. The cats had started to do what they were bred for, each catching a mouse and bringing it for her to exclaim over. Then they brought one of the beautiful bright-blue Colorado bluebirds, which she wasn't so happy about—but what could she do? That was their instinct, and she wanted them to be good hunters.

Darkness fell early, right after she'd finished her supper, and another clap of thunder echoed up and down the valley. She looked out to see Rockytop lit up by a flash of lightning. That was very close. Then the hard rain started to fall in sheets, and she decided to go to bed rather than trying to start a fire to keep warm.

The rain pounding rhythmically on the roof put her to sleep, the kittens in a vibrating pile against her back, even though it was much earlier than she usually went to bed. At first she'd tried to keep the kittens off the bed, but it really was the warmest, most comfortable place for them once they outgrew the rag-filled basket she'd fixed for them behind the stove. She laughed at the image of how horrified Edmund would be to find cats in the bed and allowed them to stay. She liked their warmth and the soft purring that often lulled her to sleep.

Sometime in the middle of the night she woke to the feeling that something wasn't right. She moved her hand on the quilt and felt moisture. Had one of the cats had an accident on the bed? Maybe it had to go and didn't want to go out in the rain. She sat up and a drop of water hit her square on the nose.

"What on earth?" she exclaimed as the fumbled for the matches and candle she kept near the bed at night. When she finally had the candle lit, she carried it to the table and lit the lantern. There was a puddle of water on the table and, as she watched, a muddy drop splashed into it from above. She looked up and realized the roof was leaking, all over. She grabbed pots and pans and began setting them under leaks, but there were more leaks than she had utensils. She moved her bed out from under the worst leak, but already muddy stains were spreading across the quilt. Everything would have to be laundered tomorrow, unless it was too rainy for things to dry. Then what?

What kind of people made a house out of logs chinked with mud? she wondered. Of course it was going to leak! What were they thinking of? Then she realized that logs and mud had probably been the only materials available when the cabin was built, since it was quite old. Honor told her it was one of the oldest in the valley, dating back to the 1880s. It had originally belonged to a long-gone homesteader, forced out by the drought. It had probably been rain-proof once. Surely there would be something that could be done to fix it.

What was it she'd heard the locals call the dirt around here? "Chico" dirt. They said that, mixed with straw and water, it made good plaster to cover the sides and roofs of the log cabins to weatherproof them. It also quickly turned to mud at the drop of a hat, or rain cloud. "Watch out when it rains," Luke had told her. "This chico dirt turns to mud and it'll mire a snake. We're more likely to be rained in around here than snowed in. There's no going anywhere if these roads get muddy."

She put on her coat, scarf, and shoes and walked carefully around the puddles over to the school, shielding the lantern from the rain, the kittens following her, lifting their paws carefully with each step. It was dry in the relatively new school building with a real roof, and she could start a fire to warm up and dry out. She'd figure out what to do tomorrow.

After a sleepless night sitting in an uncomfortable desk by the stove, Minta wasn't in a very good mood. The rain had stopped by the time she went back to her cabin to survey the damage. It was extensive. Small drips had widened to accept larger and larger streams of muddy water as chinking mud between the logs of the roof literally melted. She could see daylight through several places.

Without even taking time to make coffee, she started the long, slippery, muddy walk to Haley's place. The stream beside the road, which had almost disappeared, was now roaring with muddy runoff. She realized now why one of the rules was that the children couldn't cross the road from the school to the stream. She hadn't seen it as dangerous before, but it surely could be.

She found Fred's family just sitting down to breakfast. She knocked once and walked in, not even taking off her coat. She did undo the laces of her shoes and kicked them off with the several inches of mud they'd collected, which had made it almost impossible to walk. In fact, she'd fallen down twice, her skirt muddy where she'd caught herself on her knees. She'd dipped her muddy hands into the stream to clean them off after each time she fell.

"Fred Haley," she said before anyone had even acknowledged her presence. "You need to fix my roof. And if you don't do it today, I'm going to move my bed and my cats into the school and sleep there!"

The Haley children were staring at her in horror. She realized she must be a sight with her hair down and her clothes streaked with mud, as opposed to the neat, prim image she tried to maintain at school. Then Dale and Judy giggled at the thought of going to school and finding the teacher and her cats asleep in her bed in the middle of the classroom.

For once, Fred was speechless. His wife, Claudia, stood up and said, "Here, Minta. Robert will take your coat and scarf. Please, sit down and have some breakfast. Things always look better after breakfast. You can tell us all about it then."

Coffee had never tasted so good after her chilling trek through the mud. Minta ate some eggs, home fried potatoes, and a biscuit and was starting to feel a little better. In fact, she was starting to be embarrassed by how she'd barged in uninvited. In-between bites she filled them in on the events of her night.

After they were finished eating, Fred stood up and said, "Michael, I want you to ride over to Luke's and Jens' places and tell them we have an emergency work day at the teacherage today. Tell them to bring roofing tools and any lumber they can spare. You can stop on the way back at Paulo's, too. He'll probably help. And then get Angus and yourself over to help us. Robert, you and any of the other kids who show up can help fetch and carry things for us. I'll get my stuff and meet you there." He strode purposefully out of the room.

He still hadn't said one word to Minta. Claudia turned to her and said, "Fred's an organizer. And he's embarrassed because I told him that roof wouldn't make it through another winter. He hates it when I'm right. Not that I'd ever say, 'I told you so.'" Minta had seen the look Claudia gave Fred when she'd first come in and said her roof was leaking. Claudia didn't need to *say* "I told you so"; she *looked* it.

So, by evening, Minta had a temporary roof, awaiting the purchase of some shingling material. A *real* roof, not one made of mud.

CHAPTER TEN

Communication

❧❀❧

Saturday, October 11, 1919—*After a week-long rainy spell the end of last month, which caused some minor flash flooding along the creek, we are back to our beautiful, clear fall days.*

The aspen trees on the slopes of the LaPlata Mountains in the distance have turned bright gold, visible even from here. What it must be like to be up among them! I hope I can go there this time of year sometime. The only trees here in the valley that turn color are the fruit trees that people have planted on their places and a few cottonwoods along the stream.

I'm hoping . . .

"What now?" Minta exclaimed, capping the ink bottle but leaving her diary on the table. She ran to the door to see what all the commotion was. It sounded as if the beasts of hell had been let loose, and the cabin floor trembled as she walked across it.

About ten cows were running, bumping, and mooing their way through the schoolyard, rubbing against the side of the cabin in passing. As she stood in the doorway, one stopped and plopped a large deposit right in front of her, some of the stinky, greenish goo splashing up onto her shoes.

"That's it!" Minta screamed. "Get out of here! Shoo!" She flapped her apron at the large animal and waved her arms at it. It turned and looked at her, stuck its neck out, and mooed long and loudly. "I said, get out of here, you stupid, ugly beast!"

Hearing horse hoofbeats, she turned to see Silas ride up, his dog, Yowler, trotting along beside.

"I should have known," Minta said. "Get these ugly creatures of yours out of the schoolyard, right now!"

"Well, now, I wouldn't go calling them ugly. Stupid, I can agree with, but cows ain't ugly."

"Cows *aren't* ugly," she automatically corrected.

He smiled down at her. "I know. That's what I just said. Don't get all het up, now."

She couldn't help laughing with him.

"And, besides," he said, "they're not all mine, you know. We graze them all together here in the valley."

"Then how do you know which ones are yours?"

"They're branded, aren't they?"

"I don't know! Why don't people keep them on their own places? That's what fences are for."

"Begging your pardon, ma'am, but that's not true—not out here, anyway," Silas said as he dismounted. "We have open range. That means the cattle can go wherever they want, and anyone that doesn't want them on their property has to fence them out, not in."

"That's ridiculous. Where I come from, we keep our animals safe on our own property."

"Well, it works for out here. It takes so much ground to pasture each animal that we all need more than we've got, so all the public land is free range. In case you haven't noticed, it don't rain every five minutes here like it probably does where you came from. Where did you come from, by the way?"

"That way," she said, pointing east. "So, if I don't want cattle wandering all over the schoolyard, stepping on my pupils, and dropping their disgusting . . . droppings everywhere, I have to fence them out?"

"That's right. I suppose you could ask Fred to . . ."

She'd already thought of that, but she wasn't ready to go making more demands of Fred right after the roof. "The old fence was just made of logs cut from the piñon trees, wasn't it?" she asked.

"Looks like it," he said. "That's why it's falling apart. Piñon don't last no time at all. You need to use the cedar posts from the junipers. Building fence ain't . . . isn't too hard around here. There's plenty of raw material. Just takes some men, some muscle, and some time." She looked at him expectantly. "I guess I could go see if Paulo or anyone else wants to help. Most of the fall work's done, so we've got some time."

"Remind Paulo of what would happen if little Gina got trampled. I'm sure he'll help."

"All right," Silas sighed. "Oh, I almost forgot. Last time I was in town, Matt Post give me this for you." He reached inside his shirt and pulled out an envelope.

She frowned as she looked at the address. The return address was Constance's, but it was addressed to Minta Mayfield, care of Matthew Post, Liberty, Colorado. She hadn't wanted anyone to write her here. That's why she hadn't given anyone an address.

Silas had mounted and ridden off while she was studying the letter, so she took it inside to read. She closed the diary without finishing her entry and spread the letter's pages on the table.

Darling Minta, she read,

I know you didn't want us to write you there, but your mother was so distraught about not being able to communicate with you that I told her I'd send you a letter. Hers is enclosed. I remembered the man's name and place you sent your application to, so I took a chance on sending it there. If you've gone off someplace else, well, no harm done. Please don't be mad at me. I got the letter you mailed from somewhere in New Mexico, so maybe you did go somewhere else.

As you thought, Edmund went straight away to your parents to try to find you. Your mother said he was very unpleasant. Finally your father had to threaten to call the law to get him to leave. He left shouting, "I'll find her, and when I do I'll make her beg for forgiveness every day for the rest of her life." What a disgusting man.

Then he came to us. Fortunately, some friends of Frank's were here talking about a new business they want to start, and Edmund was out-numbered. He couldn't get too ugly, although I could tell he would have liked to. He seemed more upset about the horse and buggy than anything else. He called you, "My wife, the horse thief." He didn't believe that we didn't know where you were. But we didn't tell him anything.

Since then, I think I've seen him a few times lurking around, but he hasn't come back to the house. I hope he never comes when I'm alone. I've taken to locking the doors and windows when Frank is gone for any length of time.

But don't worry about us. You are safe, and that's what matters. Please write again when you have time; your mother begs for news of you whenever I see her.

Love, Lulu

Minta looked up, tears in her eyes, thinking of the danger she'd put her cousin in. If Edmund was "lurking around," he was probably try-ing to intercept mail. Or maybe he thought she was still in the area and would show up at Lulabelle's house eventually. But he didn't know about Constance, so it should still be safe to write through her.

Minta picked up and unfolded the next sheet of paper, the sight of her mother's spidery handwriting bringing fresh tears to her eyes.

My dearest daughter, Ella,

I know I'm supposed to call you "Minta" now, but I can't do that. You've always been our little Ella Jane. You know we were older when you were born, and we'd given up on ever being parents. Your father was determined not to spoil you since you were the only child of an older couple. But maybe we went too far and didn't tell you and show you how much we love you. Remember how he used to call you his "New Century Gal" since you were born the first week of 1900? We've both always been very proud of you.

Lulabelle says you're a teacher now. I'm sure you're a good one. I wish we had listened to you when you said you wanted to be a teacher instead of marrying Edmund, but we wanted to keep you closer to us. And I wanted you to have the security of having a husband and family. Now I know that Edmund did not provide that security for you, and I'm sorry. Please forgive us. If you can ever come back here, we will welcome you with open arms. Please continue to communicate through Lulabelle. We will accept whatever conditions you put on any correspondence, even calling you "Minta" if we have to. But you'll always be Ella in my heart.

All our love, Mother and Father

After her crying fit was over, Minta went to the water bucket and splashed cold water on her face to hide the tears. She put the folded letters in the back of her diary to answer later when she had herself under better control. Hearing approaching hoofbeats, she went out to meet Silas and Paulo.

"I agree with you, Minta," Paulo said before she'd said anything. "A schoolyard needs a good fence. There's times you don't want the kids running off everywhere, especially with the creek so close. I sent Paul up to Fred's to tell him what we're doing. If he's so inclined, he can get the rest of the community to help. Otherwise, it will just take Silas and me a little longer."

They ended up with an even larger work crew than they'd had for the roof project. Several of the wives made their husbands see the light when they thought of what might happen to kids who got under some hooves or into the creek during a flash flood. As Claudia said to Fred, "We've got a fence all around our house and yard and garden, don't we? You want your kids safe at home and not at school?" So Fred, and therefore everyone else, helped.

Fred brought a wagonload of cedar posts he'd cut and saved for fencing. When they cleared land, the farmers all burned the piñon in their stoves and saved the juniper for building. Some former resident had built the school fence out of piñon, not caring if it lasted past the few years his kids would be there.

"That's why he didn't make it here," Fred said, kicking an old piñon post that shattered into pieces at his feet. "He always did things halfway. That just doesn't work out here. If something's worth doing . . ."

"It's worth doing right," three of his kids finished for him.

At noon the women brought food to have a potluck meal in the schoolroom. By dark the fence was done except for a gate out to the road, which Jens promised to make at his house and come install when it was done. They decided against any other gates. The fence was easy to climb over if anyone needed to get out at another spot. The main thing it did was keep out large animals and define the boundaries for the kids.

"This place sure looks a lot better since you came, Minta," Sophie said to her as they surveyed the new fence. "The new roof, and now the fence. Next spring we need to start nagging Fred about a new coat of paint for the outhouses, and then we'll be looking as nice as Shady Rest."

Minta smiled at her use of the word "we," implying the school was all of theirs. And it was, really. They were like one big family. They didn't always get along, but they took care of each other, and taking care of the children was a priority for everyone. Even Silas and Mr. Rickerts, who had no kids, worked all day on the fence. If you could call leaning on a post, giving advice to everyone else "work," on Mr. Rickerts' part.

"Was I fillin' your moccasins, Silas," Rickerts called. "I'd be makin' more'n a fence for this gal. She's purtier than green grass after a drought."

Blushing, Minta walked over to where Silas was to thank him for all his help and for getting the whole project off the ground. He leaned against the fence and wiped the sweat off his forehead with his bandana, smiling at her fondly. His bluegreen eyes and sandy red hair made her think of some of the Irish kids in her practice-teaching class.

"It was no trouble," he said modestly. "I like to do things for you, Minta. In fact . . ."

She felt a tap on her shoulder and turned to see Luke.

"Could I speak with you a minute privately, Minta?" Luke said. "I'm sure Silas won't mind."

She followed him back into the school building. "Yes, what is it?" she asked.

"Well, it's about Wendell," he said, shifting from one foot to the other. "He doesn't seem to be getting the math."

"Wendell is doing fine in math," she replied.

"Maybe it was the grammar then," Luke stammered. His eyes and hair were brown, like Edmund's. Too much like Edmund's.

"Or maybe it was Florence," she said. "Or maybe you just didn't want me talking to Silas." A dark red appeared under his deep tan.

She turned her back to him and started out, reaching the door in time to see Silas riding off with Mr. Rickerts. She was surprised at how disappointed she felt.

"Don't forget, Minta," Luke said to her back. "Your contract prohibits you from keeping company with men. I hope . . ."

She whirled around. "And what are you? A sack of flour?"

"I told you. You can keep company with me because I'm on the board. I hope I don't have to bring up any inappropriate behavior between you and Silas with the other members."

"You won't," she said shortly. She walked away before she said something to him she'd regret later. "Always keep a civil tongue in your head," she could almost hear her grandmother admonishing her.

Back in her cabin, she was still fuming. Why wouldn't these men leave her alone? Sadly, she realized she didn't want Silas to leave her alone. But she couldn't lead him on, because there was nowhere it could lead. She wasn't about to become an adulterer, or a bigamist. She had been married "until death do you part" and, unless she got word of Edmund's death, she would be married to him forever.

CHAPTER ELEVEN

Trouble

༄༅༅

Wednesday, October 22, 1919—*There's definitely a fall feeling in the air. We have to use the stove in the school until past noon most days now. Nights are very cold. I've taken to putting my winter coat on top of the quilt covering me. Then I get so warm and cozy I hate to get out of bed in the morning and start the fire. I've learned to have it all set the night before, so all I have to do is light the papers under the kindling.*

I finally got a reply sent to Lulabelle and mother. Silas was going to look at a bull Mr. Rickerts was thinking of purchasing east of Durango, so I asked him to mail it there. If Edmund did intercept a letter, it would bring him dangerously close, no matter where I mail it from. I'll have to continue to rely on the name change and using Constance's address as my safeguards. And, of course, Lulabelle's silence.

I'm very worried about my folks and Lulabelle. Edmund could be very unpleasant to them if he wanted to be. He's good at going just so far—not quite far enough to bring the law into it, but far enough to cause pain and suffering. There should be a law against husbands beating their wives. I didn't even know such a thing was possible until I married him. My father would never have done that. The few times I remember my parents arguing, Father just stomped out of the house and puttered around the barn a while. Then he'd come back in and compliment Mother's cooking, or some such thing, and all would be well again. My father spanked me a few times, of course. Lulabelle and I were always doing something we shouldn't. But he wasn't mean or violent about it, and never left any marks.

Sometimes I wonder if Edmund is like he is because of how he was raised. His mother died when he was young, and his father was a harsh man with very rigid ideas about how things should be done. Edmund had some deep scarring on his back that he said was from beatings his father gave him. Well, enough! I don't want to think about Edmund, much less write about him. I'll put this away now and get my morning chores done.

Walking to school, Minta noticed a fresh blanket of white on the mountains to the north. The golden mantle of aspen was now all gone, leaving just gray rock, green pines, and now the white of snow.

"When does it usually snow here?" she asked when the kids had finished their morning exercises.

"Halloween!" Gertie shouted. "Last year it snowed on Halloween."

"Yes," Mary added. "We usually have the first snowfall around the end of October. Why?"

"I was just wondering. Soon you'll all be walking to school in the snow."

"Mostly the mud," Michael said. "It snows, but it doesn't get very cold until in January, so it melts and we have more mud than anything else."

"Lovely," Minta said, thinking of the extra cleaning all those muddy feet would bring.

After morning recess she went outside to ring the bell and had them all line up at the woodshed door instead of the school door.

"What's going on?" Florence asked.

"I've decided," Minta explained, "that, instead of having the older kids take turns to bring in wood as we've been doing, you'll all do it after every recess, since we're starting to use so much more. Angus, you come stand by me. Now hand each child as much wood as he or she can easily carry, just one piece for Gina, and so on, up to you. You and the other big kids can bring in an armload each. That way the wood box will always be full and no one person will have to do all the work."

"Especially you," Michael muttered just loudly enough for her to hear.

"Yes, Michael, especially me," she said. "We all benefit from the wood's heat, so we'll all help do the work."

"You sound just like Father," Robert said. "He's always saying we all benefit from the farm, so we have to help do the work."

At first Minta had been surprised and a little dismayed at all the farm work the kids had to do at home. But as she got to know the families and their lifestyle better, she began to see the necessity of everyone working for the benefit of all. She learned quickly not to give them much homework during busy times of the year. They had too much to do at home, and she wanted them to get their sleep. Homework was always left for the last, and they would stay up too late working on it. And the farm work they did gave them a feeling of accomplishment and self-confidence that she hadn't seen in the town kids at the school where she had practice-taught. In fact, she had learned the best way to get Angus to cooperate and behave was to give him some kind of physical work to do, like being the wood distributor at recess.

She had also set up a schedule of after-school helpers. Each day two of the students, an older one and a younger one, stayed after an extra fifteen minutes to help her sweep, clean the boards and erasers, and so forth. They liked the time spent alone with her, and the boys especially liked the job of banging the erasers together to clean the chalk out of them. They could be both violent and messy, two things they liked. The girls were less fond of that job because they got chalk dust on their clothes and in their hair, and it made them sneeze.

A few days later, Minta woke on a Saturday morning to a strange silence. The air seemed heavy somehow. She peeked out the window to see a world gone white overnight. About two inches had fallen while she was asleep. The cats ventured out, stepping gingerly in the unfamiliar substance and batting at it with their paws. The air was sharp with the spicy scent of wet sage—a smell Minta had come to love.

Shivering, Minta turned back in to the stove and bent to light the fire she'd laid the night before. She always put in a lot of wastepaper from the school with the kindling so it would light quickly and warm her up and, more importantly, boil the coffee she needed as soon as possible each morning.

The match set things ablaze immediately, but the smoke billowed back into the room instead of going up the chimney. She leaped up and checked the flue: It was open. She opened and closed it several times, but that didn't help. Meanwhile, the room was getting smokier and smokier. Her eyes were stinging with it, and she was coughing. She opened the two windows and the door and grabbed her coat, slipping into her lace-up boots without tying them.

Outside, she walked away from the house to where she could see the roof. The chimney looked like it always did, as smoke continued to boil out the door and windows. Maybe the snow had stopped it up somehow, but that didn't seem possible. Well, she wasn't going to go bother Fred again. She'd have to find someone else. She started down the road toward Valori's when she saw a lone figure on horseback approaching. She recognized Silas's brown and white dog, Yowler, trotting along beside the horse. She pulled her scarf out of her pocket and waved it to get the rider's attention.

"Silas, come here! I need you!" She impatiently waited for him to ride up, then said, before he could dismount, "There's something wrong with my stove or chimney—or something."

"Hello to you, too, Minta," he replied, tipping his hat. "Nice snow last night." He flung one leg behind the saddle and dismounted effortlessly.

Her heart was beating too fast, probably from worry about the damage the smoke was causing. "Yes, yes. Hello, Silas. I realize I'm being very presumptuous asking you to help again, but do you think you could look at my stove?"

"Like I looked at your desks and your roof and then your fence? Why is it whenever I look at something for you, it turns into an all-day job?" But he grinned as he said it.

"I'm sorry, Silas. Where were you off to this morning? Am I keeping you from something?"

"Just checking the cattle. The snow isn't too deep, so they're still able to find grass to eat, and the stream's not froze up yet. They're all right. So, let's go see about this stove of yours. Are you sure you opened the flue?" he asked condescendingly.

"Of course I opened the flue."

Silas looked at the stove and banged on the pipe while she stayed outside away from the smoke. The morning sun was warm on her back, and snow was already starting to melt on dark surfaces like the roof.

Yowler tried to approach the kittens, who were huddled under a sagebrush. Their hissing and spitting changed his mind, and he sat by the cabin door, waiting for Silas.

Silas came out and moved his horse over next to the roof and used it as a step ladder to get on top. He peered down the chimney, then came to the edge, slipping on the snowy slope, and barely stopping himself from falling. "Find me a big stick," he called down to her. "At least as long as your arm."

She had to go down to the stream and search around under some cottonwoods to find what he wanted. When she brought it back to him, he was walking carefully around the roof, looking at something.

"Here," she said, holding the stick up against the eaves so he could reach it. "What's so interesting up there?"

"Tell you when I get down," he said. "Stand back from the house now."

She moved farther away and watched as he stuck the stick down the chimney and wiggled it around. Finally, he carefully pulled it up and flung something black and smoldering off the roof into the snow below. Surely a bird couldn't have built a nest in the chimney in one day, but she couldn't imagine what else it could be.

By the time she'd walked over to it, Silas was off the roof. He prodded it with the stick, and she could tell it was gunnysack material.

"Any idea why you had a gunnysack in your chimney? Were you trying to burn it?" he asked.

"No. I don't even have any gunnysacks any more. I gave my last one to Mary when she said they needed them for the potatoes they dug this fall."

"Well, I have an idea. When I was up there I seen some footprints in the snow—little footprints."

"You mean like a raccoon or weasel or something?"

"Something like a weasel. Stay here," he ordered. He started making a circle around the cabin, staring at the ground and widening the circle when he got back to the starting point. "Aha!" he stopped.

"What?"

"Come over here," he ordered.

"All our tramping around ruined any tracks by the cabin, but I picked some up farther out. See?"

She saw two sets of footprints, one large and one small, leading away from the cabin and heading toward Rockytop Hill.

Silas whistled his horse and Yowler over to him. Then he mounted. "Stay here. I'll have the weasels for you shortly," he said.

He rode off slowly, bending down to follow the prints toward Rockytop. Minta went back inside. She built the fire back up, now that it was drawing properly, but left the windows open. It was still quite smoky inside. She put on the coffee and checked the curtains and bedding. Everything was so saturated with smoke that it would have to be cleaned and laundered. So much for getting her school chores done today.

She went back outside in time to see Silas dismount at the base of the outhouse-sized rocks that ringed the top part of the hill. His horse couldn't go any further. She hadn't climbed Rockytop yet, so she didn't know what it was like up there; but she had been told there was a dropoff on the other side. Whoever was up there was trapped. She went back inside to warm her fingers and toes by the fire. When she came out again, holding a cup of coffee, Silas was riding back. Someone was on the horse in front of him, and someone else was walking along beside, tethered by a rope from his waist to the saddle's pommel. Yowler ran circles around all of them, barking excitedly.

Minta waited, her arms folded, until they arrived.

"Caught your weasels," Silas said.

"Angus and Dale," Minta said, "what did you think you were doing?"

Dale was crying. "He said it would be a funny joke," he gasped between sobs. "He said I had to go on the woof because I was light and he could wift me up. He said it would be funny. But it wasn't, was it?" He looked down at her hopefully.

She wasn't laughing. "No, Dale, it wasn't funny."

"How about I take them over to Fred and see how funny *he* thinks it is?" Silas suggested, handing Dale down to her as he dismounted.

"He ain't home," Angus mumbled, looking at the ground. "He and Richard and Aunt Claudia went to town yesterday, and they're not coming back until tonight or maybe tomorrow now it snowed. My mom's watching all of us."

"Not very well, apparently," Minta said.

"Well, how about I take you to your mother, then? And *she* can tell Fred all about this when he does get home," Silas said.

Dale's sobs increased in intensity.

"No, Silas," Minta said. "If you don't mind, I'd like you to go tell Rachel that Angus and Dale are helping me with something and will be home later this afternoon. Tell her they'll be having lunch with me."

"Is that *all* you want me to tell her?" Silas asked, shaking his head.

"Yes, for now. Come on, boys," she said, "we've got a lot of work to do."

Silas returned in time to string a line inside the cabin to use for drying her bedding. Angus was hauling buckets of water from the well to the stove to the washtub as Dale stirred the laundry with a big stick. In-between, Angus was helping Minta scrub walls and furniture. The used water was black with smoke, and she made Angus empty it often and refill it from the water heating on the stove. He was also keeping the fire going full blast. The inside of the cabin was warm and steamy and beginning to smell like soap instead of smoke. Minta's and Angus's hands were red and chapped from the hot water.

"What can I do to help now?" Silas asked.

"Oh, Silas, you've done enough. Besides, these boys wouldn't want you to do any of the work that they should be doing, would you boys?"

Dale looked at her uncomprehendingly, not being used to sarcasm. Angus just looked down.

"How about if I fix us some lunch then?" Silas suggested. "I make pretty good potato pancakes, if you've got some potatoes and onions and eggs and flour."

"Go look in the dugout out back. There's potatoes and onions in there and I've got the rest inside. Get some apples from the barrel, too. Sliced apples go well with potato pancakes."

Minta and Silas fixed lunch while the boys continued to work under her supervision. Dale was tiring visibly. He'd probably fall asleep before they finished lunch.

"Angus," Minta said, "why were you up on Rockytop, instead of just running away where you couldn't be found?"

"We wanted to watch. There's a good view from up there."

"You know there's a rule about not climbing Rockytop. It's dangerous. What if Dale fell?"

"I was holding on to him good. It's not all that dangerous if you're careful. Except when the snakes is out. But we've had frost already, so they're back in their dens."

"Still, you broke the rule. And you caused all this mischief with my stove. So that's two strikes. The next time I *will* punish you."

"Yes, ma'am. But I kinda thought all this work was a punishment."

"Ask me," Silas said with disgust in his voice, "you should be talking to them right now with a good, sturdy willow switch. I'd be happy to fetch one for you," he offered.

Dale looked up in concern.

"Not this time," Minta said. A change of topic was in order to ease Dale's fears. "I do want to climb Rockytop. I think as soon as this snow melts, I'll do that. I'll bet the view is beautiful."

"We were going to come down and sneak off when you left to get help," Angus explained. "Only you didn't go far enough."

"And then Silas came," she added for him.

"Yeah, I knew we were dead when he started following our tracks. We shouldn'ta done it in the snow."

"You shouldn't have done it at all," she said sternly. "Why did you?"

"I don't know. We . . . I just wanted to see what you'd do, I guess. See if you could figure it out, you know."

"I still think Fred should be informed about this," Silas said.

Dale looked up again anxiously.

"I said, not this time," Minta repeated. "We'll see if they've learned anything. If they cause any more trouble, I won't be so lenient the next time. Now, Angus, come help me wring out that last sheet and get it hung up. I hope things get dry in time for me to go to bed tonight."

"Keep the fire going good and they will. And move stuff around as the ones closest to the stove get dry," Silas suggested.

"Before you leave today, Angus, I want that wood box filled to overflowing and more piled just outside the door for me."

"Yes, ma'am."

When they finally sat down to eat, potato pancakes had never tasted so good.

Chapter Twelve

Revelations

Sunday, November 2, 1919—*Since it is unseasonably warm today, after I got home from church, I put my diary, pen, and ink in my apron pockets and climbed Rockytop. The first part was easy, but when I got to the big rocks, I had to search around until I found a way up and through them. Eventually, I found a flat rock to sit on and am writing holding this diary in my lap. From here I can see the whole upper Halpern Valley. Fred's large house and Rachel's smaller one next door are to the east. Following the road west, the school and my cabin are next; and on west of that, Valoris'. Across the creek from Rachel's cabin is Luke's, and across from Valoris' is Fredricksons'—first Jens' house, then farther down the creek, his son Ernst's place. The road over the bridge continues south toward Piñon Hollow. I can see the dark spot between hills where the hollow is, but I can't see any of the buildings there, like Rickerts' or the school. Just before the road disappears into the hollow, I can see a cluster of buildings that must be the Archuleta place. That's the only home of my students I haven't been to yet. I heard Maria has been quite sick with this coming child, so I understand why they haven't invited me. Teresa said in school one day, "I'm never going to have any babies; you just throw up all the time."*

The scene is reminiscent of the play farms the little ones build in the corner of the schoolyard. The buildings look like children's blocks scattered here and there. The stream and road look like they could have been drawn by a stick; the animals grazing in clumps here and there look like pebbles.

The main road continues downstream from Fredricksons' on the other side from the school. I can't see where it meets the road to town or where Halpern Creek enters the Liberty River, but I know it's down there. It's hard to believe that the farthest away I've been since I've been here is to Halpern for church. Several times people have offered to take me to Liberty with them, but I've always begged off and just given them my shopping list and money. Eventually, I will go. The Posts have invited me to stay with them whenever I want a weekend away from school or even over Christmas. But I think I'd rather stay alone in my cabin for Christmas than with the Posts, who will have a house full of children and grandchildren whom I don't know.

The sun has warmed these rocks nicely. It's really quite pleasant sitting up here surveying my world. Such a difference from writing huddled and shivering in a dark and odoriferous outhouse. How my circumstances have changed! I wish I could build a big wall around this valley so no one could get in. But then, no one could get out, either. And where would the wall end? I wouldn't want to shut out Halpern and the church, but that's on the main road, the road that could bring Edmund here, if he ever finds out where I am.

Why do these entries so often end with Edmund? I'm determined not to think about him, but he's always in my head waiting to jump out when I least expect it. Maybe that's because he often did do the unexpected. I could never relax around him. But I can relax up here. I wish my cabin were up here. Then I could keep a lookout, and if Edmund ever came, I could . . . what? Shoot him? Jump off the cliff? Before I settled down to write, I looked over the edge to the rocks and piñons far below until I got dizzy. The truth is, I don't know what I would do if Edmund found me. I just know I will never go back to him, not even if the law says I have to, or my parents, or even the church. That's how far he's driven me. I'd even go against my church.

By the time Minta put her pen down, she was crying. She stood and brushed the dust off the back of her skirt and replaced her ink bottle, pen, and diary in her apron pockets. "When you're feeling sorry for yourself," her grandmother always said, "the best thing to do is go do something for someone else." So she'd go work on lesson plans for tomorrow. She could lose herself in the planning.

◇◇◇

She didn't write in her diary again for over a month. Every time she picked it up, she thought of Edmund and put it away quickly. She decided it was the diary itself that was bringing the unwelcome thoughts of Edmund, because it was her one link back to him—the one place that she wasn't just Minta, but Ella, too. She threw herself into her work, which wasn't hard. November was an important month at school. They were well into the year's work, and the lessons had moved from review to new concepts that took all her effort and ingenuity to teach to the students. They were also well into rehearsals for the Christmas program, refining and adding things as they got better with their lines and songs. Minta loved the creativity involved, a real chance to express herself and go beyond the confines of the set state curriculum.

She had even solved the problem of Angus, she thought. He'd been noticeably more cooperative since their Saturday spent cleaning her house from the smoke. She didn't know if that was because of her refusal to tell Fred what happened or her threat that he now had two strikes, and a third would result in some serious punishment. But whichever it was, she was enjoying the benefits.

The clothesline Silas had strung across the cabin for her to dry her sheets on had given her an idea for the play. She had Michael and Angus hang a line across the classroom about a quarter of the way back from the front, and the girls brought sheets from home that they hung for curtains, making loops at the top out of old sheeting material. Angus was in charge of opening and closing them by grabbing a handful and walking back and forth across the room. He was also in charge of changing the sets behind the curtains for different scenes and making appropriate sound effects called for in the script, all of which he enjoyed doing and did well.

She was still determined to have him do something verbal onstage, however, and broached the subject with him after school when it was his and LaQuita's turn to help clean up.

"Now that you see how much fun the play is, Angus, wouldn't you like just a small part? I could write something in for you . . ."

He was backing away from her as if she were a coiled rattlesnake. "No! I told you I won't do that!" he said.

"Why, Angus? Explain to me just what the problem is. LaQuita, take those erasers outside and see if you can clean them yourself. Well?" she asked Angus after the little girl was gone.

"I just can't get up in front of people and talk. They all look at me, and I just forget everything and get all sick in my stomach."

"But you got up in front of everyone on the cattle drive and helped herd the cattle. And you got up in front of everyone when we were fixing the fence and explained how to overlap the logs right."

"That's different. No one was looking at me expecting something. That was just stuff I do with other people every day. And besides, the people weren't looking at me when I was talking; they were looking at the cattle or the fence."

Minta mulled over Angus's words until she came up with a solution. Angus would be the announcer. He would tell what the name of the play was and, pointing to the cast, introduce the characters as each came out to center stage, as well as announce each change of scene as he pulled the curtain back for it. That way people wouldn't be looking at him. The focus would be elsewhere, but he'd still be saying enough to make his mother and uncle feel he had a real part in the play. He reluctantly agreed to try her idea in rehearsals and, to his surprise, found he liked doing it. He wasn't so sure he'd still like it when they did it in front of people, though.

One Sunday after church Claudia invited Minta for dinner. Various families often did that, now that she was attending regularly and playing the piano most Sundays. Claire Carpenter was pleased to be able to take a break from a job she'd been doing for several years. Minta appreciated the chance to get out of her cabin and enjoy someone else's cooking. After they ate, the children whose turn it was to do the dishes began clearing the table, and the others went out for late afternoon chores with Fred. Minta and Claudia sat in the two rocking chairs beside the stove.

"I thought about inviting Luke today, too, Minta," Claudia said, "but I wasn't sure how you'd feel about it."

"Oh, I'm glad you didn't. You know my contract forbids me to keep company with men."

Claudia laughed. "Oh, *that!* They always put that in so young women don't come out here looking for husbands. But they don't expect you to be an old maid. You can get married if you wait until summer. You can even keep teaching when you're married unless you . . . you know . . . are in the family way."

"That's what my grandmother called it: 'the family way.' She didn't even like the term 'expecting,' much less 'pregnant.' But I'm not going to get married, and I certainly won't be in the family way. I wish Luke would stop pursuing me."

"Why? I know he's quite a little older than you, but he's got his own place. He's really a fine man. One of the best, Fred says—and Fred doesn't give praise lightly. Is it because of Silas? I know he's sweet on you, too."

"Stop, Claudia," Minta said, blushing. "No, it's not because of Silas, and I don't want anyone to be sweet on me. I came here to teach, and that's all."

"Your devotion to your profession is admirable, Minta, but surely you don't plan on living alone your whole life. Don't you want children?"

"I *have* children. *Fourteen* of them!"

"You know what I mean, Minta. What about when you're old and sick? Who will take care of you if you have no real children or grandchildren?"

"I can't worry about that now. I have enough problems getting through each day as it comes. 'Don't borrow trouble from tomorrow,' my grandmother used to say. Actually, she would probably quote the Bible in this situation—Matthew 6:34, one of her favorites: 'Take therefore no thought for the morrow; for the morrow shall take thought for the things of itself. Sufficient unto the day is the evil thereof.'" Minta looked down as she finished reciting. The evil thereof, indeed. Her lies were perpetuating the evil.

"You talk about your grandmother a lot, Minta. She must have been a special woman," Claudia said.

"Oh, she was! She helped raise me. She lived with us, and my folks were always so busy working that I spent most of my time with her."

"Where was that, Minta? I just realized I don't know where you came from."

Minta looked at her hands in her lap. She couldn't lie to this woman who was so kind to her. She couldn't answer her, either. So she did what she always did: changed the subject.

"That was a lovely meal, Claudia. Thank you so much. And thank you for not inviting Luke without asking me first. That was thoughtful of you."

"So Luke really has no hope with you?" Claudia asked after waiting to see if Minta would go on.

"No, he doesn't," Minta said as she looked up, determined to keep to her fiction. "Why doesn't he court your sister-in-law, Rachel? She's not much older than he is, is she?"

"No. Not much. But Rachel's . . . Well, you didn't know her before. She's a lot better now."

"I hardly know her now. She seldom talks to me at meetings. Better than what?"

"Well, after Richard, Fred's brother, died—our Richard is named after him, you know—after he died, Rachel just didn't come out of it. Part of it was how he died, so sudden and so useless. He'd made it through a year of the war with only minor wounds, just enough to get him sent home. He was healing nicely and very optimistic about the future. One day he was riding home from Valoris', and right past the school a snake spooked the horse. It jumped sideways and threw him off. His head hit a rock and he died instantly. Angus saw the whole thing. He was on his way to meet his dad and got there just in time to see him die."

"How awful," Minta mumbled, unable to think of anything more appropriate to say. She had read recently, and passed on to her students, that the Great War—the War to End All Wars—had resulted in ten million men's deaths worldwide, 115,000 of them from the United States. How ironic that a man could survive that and then die almost on his own doorstep.

"Yes. Rachel just went into a shell. She couldn't keep house or take care of the kids. Just sat in a chair and rocked for hours and hours. Fred promised he'd take care of her and the kids, and he has. But finally, I couldn't stand her kids coming over hungry and dirty all the time, and I went over there one day and physically made her get up and get to work. That was over a year ago, and she's gotten gradually better since then. But she says she'll never look at another man. Richard was so kind and so good that no one else will ever be good enough. I think Luke knows that."

"And I guess she doesn't need a man if she's got Fred to be a surrogate father and husband."

"No, *she* doesn't, Minta. What's *your* excuse?"

Minta didn't answer, thinking of poor Angus and Mary. It explained a lot about their early behavior at school. But Mary had come out of her shyness and taken on her role of oldest female student, excelling academically and bossing the younger ones at recess, helping dry tears and blow noses. Now, if only Angus would make some similar gains, she'd feel like she'd done her job as their teacher. The better she got to know these children, the more she realized how much she didn't know about them. They each had a story, and she had come in in the middle of it, not knowing the beginning or the ending. Just like her. She had a story, too. She knew the beginning, but she was afraid to think what the ending might be.

"Minta, are you all right?" Claudia asked. "The funniest look just crossed your face."

"Yes . . . I was just thinking about . . . something. Claudia, can I ask you a rather embarrassing question? I hope you won't be offended. I don't mean to be offensive."

"Certainly, Minta. What is it?"

"Well, how did you . . . do you . . . stand to have so many kids? I mean, isn't it really painful and . . ."

Claudia laughed as Minta stumbled over her words. "Ah, yes. I forget you've never been married. Didn't your mother talk to you about these things?"

"She just said, 'I'm sure you know you need a man to have children.' That was . . ." Minta stopped herself from saying "right before I got married" and changed it to ". . . the only thing she told me about childbearing."

Claudia laughed. "Well, that part's true. You *do* need a man. That's the good part. And, sure, childbirth is painful, but you forget the pain quickly. And after the first one, it usually gets easier."

"I know childbirth is painful. I meant the . . . the conception. Isn't that painful, too? What did you mean about the 'good part'? How could something like that be good?"

"Minta! Where do you get such funny ideas?" Claudia blushed before adding, "It's not painful—in fact, just the opposite. Well, I guess maybe the first time there was a little pain, but that was nothing compared to . . . . It's, well, it's quite pleasant. Oh, that's not a good word for it. I don't know the right word. You'll just have to get married and find out. If fear of childbirth or conception is what's been holding you back, I can tell you from *much* experience with both that you have nothing to worry about."

"Thank you for answering my questions so honestly, Claudia. I know it was embarrassing for you. Why don't women ever talk about these things?"

"I don't know. I'm going to tell my daughters what's what well before they are old enough to get married. I didn't know a thing before I got married either, except what I saw animals do. My wedding night was quite the learning experience, let me tell you. But I think girls should know beforehand, don't you?"

"Oh, yes, I agree, Claudia. The more they know before, the better. It could keep them from making some awful mistakes."

CHAPTER THIRTEEN

Celebration

❧❦❧

Friday, December 19, 1919—*I'm so nervous I can hardly write. But at least I won't write about "him." I've got too much else on my mind. Tonight is the Christmas program. Ever since Honor said it was the time the community would judge me, I've been getting more and more worried. Practices have been going well, and the kids are happy and excited, but I'm second-guessing myself. What if people don't approve of my doing a play instead of the more traditional program they usually do? What if someone objects to my taking the Christmas story and setting it in the Old West? Is that against the Bible? Well, it's too late now. Tonight will come soon enough, and what happens, happens. I do hope the other surprise I have in store for everyone works out.*

It snowed a little yesterday; today is clear and cold. I was afraid the roads would be too snowy or muddy for people to get here, but it looks like it will be all right. The roads are frozen mud, and the wind isn't blowing to drift the snow. We're going to take a month off school now, maybe more, depending on the weather. Several families invited me for Christmas, and I'm going to Haleys' for Christmas Eve and then to Valoris' on Christmas afternoon. I can walk to both of those places, so no one will have to come get me or take me home. After that, I don't know what I'll do. If I can get a ride to Liberty, I suppose I'll spend a few days with Posts', shopping and visiting the library for more teaching materials and ideas.

Writing isn't easing my nervousness. I might as well go over to the school and get things ready.

The school was packed to overflowing. Wagons, buggies, and horses lined up outside. Light from several lanterns spilled out of the windows and onto the frozen ground. Minta took one last look around her cabin to make sure all was ready for "Santa's" arrival. She patted her hair into place one more time, smoothed down her good church skirt which didn't need smoothing, took a deep breath, picked up her lantern, and walked over to the school, smiling and greeting the few still arriving.

There were several people there she didn't know, and she smiled at Matthew Post and his wife, Miriam. The four schools in the district had all agreed to schedule their programs for different nights so families could attend each other's if they wanted to. Some whom she recognized from church had come from Piñon Hollow and Halpern. Maybe the people she didn't know were from Shady Rest. Most of those people went into Liberty for church.

Inside, the desks, chairs, and benches had been lined up for the audience. Women were seated first. Minta smiled to see Alice Fredrickson, Jens' daughter-in-law, seated sideways in one of the large desks to accommodate her large bulk. There was some talk of her maybe having twins, since they ran in the family and because she was so large. Whatever she was having was due any day now. Alice reminded Minta of Maria Archuleta, and she looked around for her. Archie was standing by himself off to one side, so Maria must still be too sick to come. Or maybe she was like Minta's grandmother and didn't think a woman should show herself in public in that condition. Her baby was due in late January, the worst time to have a child out here. It was hard to get the doctor in or the patient out, if needed.

The children in the audience sat in front of everyone on the floor. Standing men lined the walls. Minta had added wood to the stove an hour ago, but now she realized the room was so hot they'd have to let the fire burn down. All those bodies crowded in together in their winter clothes produced enough heat.

Minta checked on her students waiting in anticipation behind the curtain, trying to be quiet but unable to contain their nervous energy.

The sooner she got this show on the road the better, she realized as she glanced from face to nervous face. She looked at Angus. He was both pale and ruddy—pale skin with bright red spots on his cheeks. He was twisting a piece of his shirttail in one hand.

"Tuck in your shirt, now, Angus," she said calmly. "Remember what I told you. Don't look directly at anyone except for me. Look above their heads or at a spot on the wall. Just say your lines as you do the curtain like we practiced. Everything will be fine." He nodded uncertainly and swallowed. "Is everyone else ready? Okay, Angus, you come out with me and take up your position." As they stepped through the curtain, the talking, laughing, and scuffling died down to just a few whispers, shushes, and coughs. Angus stood on the left side while Minta stayed in the middle.

"Good evening," she said. "Welcome to Rockytop School. We're very happy you could all come tonight." And so the long-awaited evening began. After her introductory remarks, Minta took her place at the piano and nodded to Angus.

He stuttered and stammered a little bit, eyes downcast, but got through the introduction of the play and began on the cast. As each child was introduced, and he realized everyone was looking at that child instead of at him, his voice became more confident and his head came up. When everyone was lined up, Minta began playing, and the children sang the first song, "Oh Little Town of Bethlehem." Then Angus closed the curtain again, waited for the scrambling on stage to settle down, and announced the first scene.

After that, things went so fast that Minta wasn't sure they had done everything as planned. She was watching the kids, playing for the intermittent songs, smiling encouragingly at Angus whenever he had to talk, and trying to listen to the audience's reactions—all at once. At least they seemed to be laughing in the right places, and they applauded every song and every scene ending with vigor.

The hit of the show was Robert, who stole every scene he was in as the angel Gabriel. He was dressed in white cowboy hat, shirt, and pants and was riding a stick horse to which he'd yell "whoa" and "giddyup," just like a real one. Mary was a charming Mary, her blond hair hidden beneath a blue scarf and clutching her doll wrapped in kitchen toweling swaddling clothes. Michael was convincing as the carpenter, Joseph, working in his shop; and the others, as the townspeople, managed to stumble their way through a fairly convincing square dance at the celebration of Mary and Joseph's engagement.

Before she knew it, Angus was pulling the sheets back for the final curtain call. She and Angus joined the ends of the lineup, and they all bowed together. Then they all stepped back, Angus closed the curtain, and Honor introduced herself and began playing her piano piece. While Honor was playing, Minta went to each beaming student and hugged and whispered compliments to each one. Last was Angus. She wasn't sure he'd welcome a hug, but he didn't resist; and she whispered, "What a good job you did, Angus. I'm proud of you."

"It was okay," he said, trying not to smile, but she saw the grin as he turned away from her.

Honor's song ended, and they opened the curtains for the final time to join the crowd in the room waiting to congratulate and compliment the children. When Minta finally allowed herself to look at individuals in the audience, she was relieved to see they were smiling and anxious to talk to her and the kids.

"Oh, Minta," Claudia said as she worked her way through the crowd. "Heavens to Betsy, that was wonderful! Where did you ever find that script? I thought Old Man Rickerts was going to fall over laughing when Robert came out the first time riding on that stick horse and acting like the angel Gabriel. I overheard him say, 'She musta bin hard up fur angels to put that boy in white!'"

"Miss Mayfield wrote the script, Mother," Honor said. "It was so hard not to tell you all about it while we were working on it."

"I was beginning to wonder if you were having a program at all, you were all so close-mouthed about it. Now I see why," Claudia replied. "Oh, there's Rachel signaling me. I need to help get these refreshments set up. No, no, Minta. You don't need to help. People want to talk to you."

Soon everyone was sitting or standing, munching on homemade Christmas cookies and fudge and drinking hot spiced apple cider from a big pot on the stove. Someone had added a little wood to keep the fire from going out completely, and a pleasant odor of apple, cinnamon, and cloves rose with the steam from the pot.

Minta sat at her desk, which had been moved to the back corner, and sipped a cup of hot cider. Honor, followed by several of the other kids, came up to her, holding presents. Minta opened the one from Honor first—a green scarf carefully hemmed with tiny stitches. After admiring Honor's sewing ability, she opened a clumsily wrapped package from Michael and Angus. It was a bird that Angus had carved out of aspen wood and Michael had painted.

"I didn't know you boys were so artistic," she said. "This is beautiful. I'll treasure it always."

Gradually, Minta became aware of the worried looks among the kids. Finally, Mary came up to her, "Mr. Rickerts is still sitting there eating, ma'am. Shouldn't you tell him it's time to get ready to . . . you know?"

"Let's give him a few minutes, Mary. He needs to enjoy the refreshments, too."

"But usually Santa comes by now. The little kids are getting worried," Mary whispered, making sure none of the younger children could hear her.

"Excuse me, Mary, but it looks like Mr. Post wants a word with me." Minta stood and walked away, leaving the confused girl to whisper her concerns to the other big kids.

After a few more minutes, even the adults were looking anxiously at Rickerts, wondering why he was dilly-dallying around. Minta would have to do something before someone confronted him.

She walked up to the piano. "Let's all sing a Christmas carol," she shouted into the noise of the crowd. They settled down when they heard the first few notes of "Silent Night." She started over and they all fell in singing lustily, the male voices harmonizing nicely with the women's higher pitches. They were almost done with the last verse when the cloakroom door burst open and a man dressed in a red suit stepped in, carrying a large sack and shouting, "Merry Christmas! Ho, ho, ho!"

There was total silence for a moment as everyone looked from the stranger to Mr. Rickerts, who continued to chew on a cookie to hide his grin, pretending he didn't know everyone was looking at him.

Minta found Mary's face in the crowd, and she'd gone pale. Soon a knot of the older kids was whispering together as the younger ones crowded around Santa to get their goodies. Minta walked over to them and heard Robert say, "But all the men are here, even Mr. Rickerts and Mr. Post. Who else can it be?"

"It has to be the *real* Santa," Florence asserted. "There's no other explanation."

"I told you so, Gunner," Gertie said. "It is *too* him."

Gunny frowned but didn't have an answer.

"You kids go line up now to get your presents from Santa," Minta ordered.

After all the gift bags had been distributed, the stranger in red yelled, "Ho, ho, ho! Merry Christmas!" again and backed out of the room. Minta stood in the doorway so no one would try to follow.

"Who was that, Uncle Fred?" Minta heard Mary asking.

"You got me," he answered.

"I can't imagine," Rachel was saying to Sophie as Minta walked back into the crowd.

Santa's departure meant the evening had come to an end, and families began gathering up their children, coats, dishes, and lanterns. Minta stood at the door like a preacher after church, shaking hands and accepting compliments from people as they left. Now that it was all over, she had a headache and just wanted to go home to bed.

"Well done, Minta," Matthew Post said as he left. "People will be talking about this one for a long time to come. We hope to see you in town over winter vacation."

"Yes, I'll come if I can get there."

"Why don't you just come with us tonight?" Miriam asked. "We'd love to have you. You can stay as long as you like."

"Thank you, but I'm spending Christmas with some families here."

"That's good," Matthew said. "I'm happy to see you're becoming part of the community. Even Fred has quit complaining so much about all your newfangled ideas, although he still feels you could be a stricter disciplinarian."

"I'm trying," Minta said, too tired and headachy to argue.

Finally they were all gone, and Minta blew out the last two lanterns and closed the door on the mess. She'd deal with it later. She had at least a month.

She opened her cabin door and stepped into the dark. Why hadn't she thought to bring her lantern from the school? Something told her she wasn't alone, and she drew in her breath, hesitant whether to run or confront whoever it was. Then the flare of a match lit up a man sitting on the bed as he lit her candle.

"Edmund, no!" Minta gasped, stumbling backwards and banging her backbone painfully on the door jam. Even as she said it, she realized it wasn't so. The candle flame took hold, and she recognized Silas, as well as the pile of red clothing on the bed.

"What are you doing here?" she asked much more sharply than she intended. "You scared me to death!"

"Sorry. But I didn't want any light, so the kids wouldn't see anyone was over here as they left. Who's Edmund?"

"I thought you'd be long gone by now, Silas." Minta ignored his question. "But, thank you. You did a great job. No one, not even the adults, had a clue it was you. I'll bet we caused a lot of people to keep believing in Santa Claus."

"Yeah, spreading around that story about going down to Waterflow to see a rancher I used to work for was a stroke of genius. No one thought I was around." He paused before he repeated, "Who's Edmund?"

"You can't be here, Silas. My word! It's after ten o'clock! Do you want to get me fired?"

"Not even Fred would dare fire you because of Santa Claus," he said, picking up the beard he'd discarded on the bed and brushing it playfully across her face. "Besides, who comes and checks to make sure you don't have any men in your cabin at night?"

"No one. But that's not the point. *I* know you're here. And I want you to leave!"

"Do you really? Or just so I won't ask you who Edmund is again?"

"I'd appreciate it if you'd forget you ever heard that."

"Okay. And I, Santa, would appreciate a kiss for Christmas," Silas leaned toward her, circling her shoulders with his arm.

She tried to squirm away, but he was too strong. She turned her head in time, though, and the kiss aimed for her mouth landed instead on the side of her neck. She panicked. The arms holding her, the male smell, the hot breath on her face brought back unpleasant memories. Suddenly she was desperate to get away.

A sharp elbow in Silas's ribs had the desired effect, and he let her go, stepping back in confusion. "Calm down, Minta," he said.

"Don't you ever do that again," Minta ordered in her teacher voice. "I mean it. I thought you were going to . . . to hurt me." Hot tears slid down her face, and she brushed them away with a sleeve.

"I would never hurt you, Minta. I'm sorry. I won't do anything you don't want me to, but you've got to talk to me. Tell me what you want."

No man had ever spoken to her so kindly. She wanted more than anything to melt into his arms and let him hold her gently, as she knew he'd be capable of. But she couldn't. Not in the mess she'd made of her life. Instead, she had to answer his question.

"I already told you," she said as coldly as she could manage. "I want to be left alone."

"I don't believe that. You do make it real hard for a man to court you, though, Minta."

"I don't want to be courted." Minta stepped back to keep him at arm's length.

"I'm not good enough for you? I guess I can understand that, you being a educated lady and all. I had to quit school after seventh grade, but the teacher said I had a right good head on my shoulders."

"Oh, Silas, it's not that. It's not you."

"Must be that Edmund feller, then. Don't even know who he is, but I don't like him. He sounds like a mangy devil to me."

Minta couldn't help laughing. "You got that right. But I meant what I said. You have to forget you ever heard that name and never talk about him to me again. Is that clear?"

"Yes, Teacher. That's clear. Like Rickerts says, 'Never argufy with a woman.'"

"It's obvious by your tone you don't appreciate being talked to like a student. But this is who I am. Maybe you don't want to court me after all." She held the door open for him.

"Maybe. But I doubt it," Silas said as he left. She didn't hear his comments as he mounted his horse: "It'd be easier tracking a shadow in the rain. Come on, Yowler. Good thing she don't know how stubborn I am."

CHAPTER FOURTEEN

Survival

✌❀✌

Thursday, January 8, 1920—*My plans to go to Liberty have gone awry. The weather turned bad just after Christmas, and there is no going anywhere except by foot or horseback. I don't want to go that far either way this time of year. I kept busy this past week giving the school a good cleaning and getting lessons ready for the rest of the school year. But it was too hard keeping both buildings heated, so now I'm here in my small cabin trying to find things to do. Just surviving—bringing in wood, keeping the worst of the snow off the paths, trying to stay warm—takes a lot of my time.*

Christmas was pleasant enough with the Haleys and Valoris, but I found myself missing home and family more than I expected. Not Edmund or his house, of course, but the home of my childhood. Seeing the children enjoying Christmas reminded me of so many from my past with Lulabelle and my parents and grandparents and aunts and uncles. I wonder how they all spent the holiday and if my disappearance caused them unnecessary pain. I know how Edmund spent Christmas: just like any other day. He isn't one for celebrating. But, I determined not to write of him in here any more, so I won't.

A happy event occurred the day after Christmas. Alice and Ernst had a baby boy. Almost ten pounds! No wonder she was so large. Fortunately, there were no complications with just Hannah and Claudia in attendance. They named him James. Their girl Lilly is two. Gunner will be so happy to have a boy to go with Gertie's little Lilly. I'm glad we have some time off school right now. I'm sure the twins are so excited that that's all we'd hear about. Seeing these big happy families here makes me realize what I missed by being an only child. I wish I could have had children of my own, but that brings me back to where I determined not to go. It must be time to close for today, dear diary.

Another storm blew in that night, and Minta woke to fresh drifts of snow across the pathways she'd cleared the day before. She was just finishing uncovering her path to the woodshed when she heard horses and voices. She looked up to see Michael and Angus riding toward her, the horses picking their way carefully through the snow, steam rising from their nostrils.

"Miss Mayfield," Michael yelled as soon as they were close enough. "You have to come with us to help."

"Come inside and warm up," she told the boys as they dismounted. "Help what? What's wrong?"

"It's Mrs. Archuleta, ma'am," Michael explained. "She had her baby too early, and now she's really sick. They got the doctor out here by meeting him in Halpern with Father's sleigh, but he says they have to take her all the way to Durango to the Sisters of Mercy Hospital."

"How can I help?" Minta asked.

"With the girls. Mother wondered if maybe you could stay and take care of the Archuleta girls. It might be for several days or even longer. Come on, they said to hurry. You can put what you need to take in my saddlebags. You can ride my horse—she's real gentle—and I'll ride with Angus."

"Of course," Minta said, thinking fast. She put her diary, ink and pen, Bible, comb and brush, hair pins, nightgown, and change of clothes in the bags. What else? She looked around and added a few books she could read to the girls.

"Oh, dear," she said, almost stepping on Blackie. "What about my cats?"

"You could leave some food and water for them. If you're gone very long, I'll come check on them," Angus said.

Minta filled a large pan with water and set it on the floor. Then she took the pot of oatmeal she'd made that morning and set it down, too. It would last them a while. She added a few pieces of bread and meat scraps she'd been saving for lunch. It was silly to worry about cats at a time like this, but she'd grown fond of them. They wouldn't understand why their source of food and warmth was gone.

"I'm afraid their water will freeze," she said.

"I'll come check on them, ma'am. Don't worry about it," Angus said again.

"Thank you, Angus. I know I can count on you."

"Dress warm, I mean warmly, ma'am. There's really a cold wind out there," Michael said.

She knotted her wool scarf so it wouldn't come undone and added another pair of socks before she put her outside boots back on and laced them up. Her winter coat and gloves completed her preparations. Michael already had the saddlebags on and held his mare while Angus helped her mount.

She was thankful for the scarf as the wind whipped her face and even more thankful that Michael's horse just followed Angus's with no direction from her, so she could turn her face away from the wind. Even so, her ears and toes felt frozen by the time they arrived at the Archuleta homestead.

She had never been there before and was surprised by how much was there. Besides the cabin and outhouse, there were several outbuildings and corrals for various animals. She realized most of the horses in the yard belonged to neighbors who had come to help. Someone was hitching a horse to a sleigh as they arrived. It would be the only mode of transportation that would work today. She saw a mattress and quilts piled on the floor between the seats, ready to transport the patient.

She dismounted and walked stiffly into the warm cabin filled with women talking in hushed tones. The doctor was putting on his coat. "The baby would never survive the trip," he was saying. "I doubt the poor little thing will survive anyway without mother's milk, but you can try. I see they've got goats out there. Try warm goat's milk every two hours. If he can't keep that down, ask the neighbors for some cans of Borden's."

"I've got a better idea," Hannah said. "I'll go get my daughter-in-law. She just had a baby and can wet nurse."

"Oh, Hannah, are you sure?" Sophie asked. "She needs her milk for little James."

"Her body will just make more. I raised twins, didn't I? I know how it works."

"Good idea," the doctor said. "But best take the baby to her. She can take better care of him in her own place. Wrap him up good and get him there as fast as you can. And he looks a little jaundiced. Try to get him some sunlight as soon as possible."

"Jens," Hannah was already yelling to the men outside, "get ready. We need to go."

Minta looked around and finally saw the three little Archuleta girls huddled by the stove, watching and listening with big, scared eyes. She sank to the floor in front of them.

"Hello, girls," she said. "I came to stay with you. The doctor will take care of your mother. The Fredricksons will take care of your new baby. And I will take care of you. Okay?"

"Is Jaime going to be all right?" LaQuita asked.

"If all the people who want to help can do anything about it," Minta said. "God willing," she added.

"I'm worried about Mama," Teresa said, tears running down her face. "There was a lot of blood. I had to stay with her while Papa went for help. She couldn't even talk to me."

They all looked up as Archie carried his wife through the room, wrapped in a blanket, her long dark hair spilling over his shoulder. She moaned but didn't open her eyes. The doctor opened the door for him and they disappeared.

"Papa didn't even say goodbye," LaQuita said. "Where are they taking Mama?"

"They're taking her to the hospital," Minta said. "We'll just have to pray for her and take care of things here as best we can. We can do that, can't we, girls?"

"We have a lot of animals," LaQuita volunteered. "Horses, and a cow, and chickens, and two sheep, and three goats, and a pig."

"Well, we'll take good care of them, won't we?" Minta said, drawing Wanda onto her lap.

Hannah approached with a bundle in her arms. "Minta? I thought the girls would want to say goodbye to their little brother. Jaime, is it?"

"Yes, but it's 'Hi-may,'" Teresa emphasized the Spanish pronunciation. "That's Spanish for James. Isn't that your new grandbaby's name?"

"Yes, we'll have two little Jameses at our place for a while," Hannah said. "Say goodbye now, girls." Hannah bent down so they could see the tiny, reddish-yellow face. Minta knew that Hannah was thinking this might be a final goodbye, but she didn't want to scare the girls.

Teresa burst into tears. "I want my baby brother to stay here. I'll take care of him. I promised Mama."

Minta hugged her. "He needs real mother's milk, honey. He can get that with the Fredricksons. As soon the weather clears up, I'll take you down to visit him. You can walk that far, can't you?"

"LaQuita and I can. I don't know about Wanda."

"Then I'll carry her on my back. We'll all go see him as soon as we can."

Teresa gently planted a teary kiss on the black fuzz of the little head, and Hannah rose.

"Thank you for coming to help, Minta. One of us could have taken the girls in, but someone has to stay here and care for the place, and the girls know best where everything is and what needs to be done."

"Of course I came to help," Minta said. "That's what we do here."

❖ ❖ ❖

If Minta had thought survival at her cabin was complicated, it was nothing compared to the Archuletas' place. The big kitchen stove had to be kept going day and night for heating and cooking. All the animals had to be fed and watered and the ice kept chipped out of their water troughs. The cow was dry right now, but two of the goats had to be milked. The water had to be carried in buckets across treacherous, frozen ground. Little girls had to be hugged and read to and reassured that they would get their own lives back someday, that this strange existence was only temporary.

If there was a bright spot in the whole thing, Minta thought, it was that the girls were really opening up to her in a way they never had in school, telling her about their lives and their hopes and dreams. Even Wanda, to whom she'd been a complete stranger, kept as close to her as possible, craving attention. It took two days to get things organized to where she thought they were doing all that needed to be done, and then Teresa asked again about going to see Jaime.

It hadn't snowed again and the sun was out. The fact that no one had come bringing bad news told her the baby was still alive, so she bundled the girls up and began the trek downhill to the Fredricksons'. The road was soft and muddy in the middle, but if they stayed to the sides, the walking wasn't too bad. Hannah saw them coming and came out onto the porch to wave them on to Ernst's cabin downstream.

An exhausted-looking Alice was sitting in a rocker, two babies in her arms—one asleep, one fussing. Minta dropped her coat and reached for the fussy one, James, and instinctively began walking and talking to him in a soothing voice. When he had settled, she looked over her shoulder, and all three girls were bent over Jaime, watching him nurse. He had woken up when Minta took James and instinctively searched for a nipple. His little fist was curled around Teresa's finger while LaQuita stroked his arm with her finger. Wanda stared wide-eyed, her thumb in her mouth.

Alice smiled up at Minta. "I'm so glad you came today, Minta," she said. "Hannah's been helping me, but she finally went home to take care of her own house for a while. I don't know how she handled two babies by herself out here. It's all I can do just to keep them fed, much less changed and bathed. And poor Ernst hasn't had a hot meal since . . . ," she stopped, looking at the little girls admiring their brother.

"You do look tired, Alice. When you're done feeding him, let us take over for a while and you go take a nap."

"A nap! That would be wonderful, but it's about the time Lilly wakes up from her nap. She's been very cranky lately with two new babies taking up everyone's time and attention."

"We'll take care of Lilly, too, when she wakes up. I'll bet Wanda would play with her, wouldn't you, honey?" Minta asked. Wanda nodded, thumb still in her mouth.

"Maybe all the kids could play on the porch in the sun, and you could hold Jaime out there in the rocker. It's warm enough for him to get some more sun. I think he already looks a little less yellow," Alice said.

"Yes, we can do that. Put your coats back on, girls," Minta instructed.

"Can I hold Jaime in the rocker?" Teresa asked. "Then you could hold James."

"All right," Minta said. "You and LaQuita can take turns holding him if you're very careful."

"Can you come every day?" Alice asked, smiling.

"Oh, yes! Please can we, Miss Mayfield?" Teresa asked. "I'll get up earlier and do extra work at home, so we can get all the chores done in time."

"That won't be necessary, Teresa. I think we can do both, as long as the weather stays good so we can walk safely. Let's see what all we can do here to help Alice."

So a routine was established: breakfast, morning chores, lunch, walk to Alice's, baby-sit, walk back, evening chores, dinner, reading time, bed. The days were full and tiring, but the girls were thriving on the exercise and excitement of getting to hold Jaime and help with his care. Little Wanda often had to spend the time at Alice's napping, but even she got so she could walk all of the way down. Minta still had to carry her most of the way back up the hill, though.

Minta realized she was doing even harder and dirtier work than Edmund had made her do, but she didn't mind it. She had bruises again, too, but from an uncooperative goat—a *real* one, not the two-legged variety. When the girls came running from their chores one evening shouting that their papa was coming, she was almost sorry her time there was about to come to an end.

Archie and Fred, who had driven them from town, helped Maria into the house. Archie said she had been badly anemic after giving birth; but they fed her a lot of liver in the hospital, and she was getting stronger. She was pale and unsteady on her feet, but at least she was walking and able to greet the girls with hugs and kisses before she went to bed.

The next morning Archie fetched Jaime home, and the family was complete again. Minta stayed two more days to help Maria, but with Archie there to take care of the chores, the girls such good helpers, and Maria getting stronger every day, she was no longer needed.

Maria's milk had dried up during her hospitalization, so Alice came up every morning, and Archie took Jaime down to her house every evening to nurse. In-between they gave him goat's milk. Soon, Jaime would be completely weaned to the goat's milk. Alice, who at first hadn't wanted the extra burden, told Minta she was sorry to see him go. She thought it might be all right if her next pregnancy did result in twins.

Minta thought of James and Jaime as twins in spirit and hoped they would grow up that way, safe in this valley so far from the prejudices of the outside world. She went back to her cabin determined to be a better teacher than ever and to always put the best interests of her students first. They might live in a world that allowed men to die falling off horses, women to suffer in childbirth, wives to be beaten, and people's color or culture to make a difference in how they were treated, but in her school, they would be safe and happy and well educated and, yes, even well disciplined. It was the least she could do for these people who took care of both her and each other.

CHAPTER FIFTEEN

A Very Bad Day

Sunday, January 25, 1920—*I finally made my trip to Liberty, riding in with the Valoris and back with Silas. In Indiana, I would have thought Liberty an impossibly small town, but it seemed very prosperous and bustling with several new businesses opening up. I stayed four days with the Posts and made the most of my time. I spent one day at the library and talked the librarian into letting me keep some books longer than normal, so I can read them to the students. I spent another day-and-a-half at the Liberty School, observing classes and visiting with the teachers. Now that I feel I know what I'm doing, I was brave enough to ask them questions about how they handle certain situations and problems.*

The four different teachers were quite interesting. The first and second grades' teacher was an older woman who has been teaching a long time. She kept the kids quiet in straight, bolted-down rows and required a lot of memorization. The third and fourth grades' teacher was a woman my age, also in her first year of teaching. Her room was a mess, the students out of control. Of course she has twenty-three students in two grades, and I'll admit fourth graders can be very trying, but still! It was all I could do to sit there and not interfere. All it would have taken was a firm hand. The fifth and sixth grades' teacher was my favorite. She was middle-aged and allowed the kids some freedom in the classroom, but she still kept order and got a lot done. The only man was the seventh and eighth grades' teacher. He was most helpful to me, as I'm starting to worry about Angus passing the eighth grade exam next year. He gave me sample exams and some tips on how to teach him to handle the testing experience in a big school with people he doesn't know.

I was afraid things with Silas would be awkward on our ride home. I think they would have been, but he was worried about Mr. Rickerts, who got sick right after Christmas and is still doing poorly. Silas had picked up some medicine in town for him. When he dropped me off at my cabin, he just said, "I haven't forgotten I'm courting you, Minta. Don't you forget it, either." He didn't allow me to respond—just urged his horse on and waved without turning around. Men!

Now I must get ready to start school up again. Since there have been no more big storms, I plan on reopening school tomorrow. I didn't realize how much I missed it until I was sitting in the classes in Liberty, wishing I was with my own students. I especially miss the Archuleta girls. I got so close to them during my stay there.

Minta had picked up two letters at Matthew's while she was in Liberty. The one from her mother was short and to the point: They missed her at Christmas, and Uncle Willard died. Minta hadn't been close to her uncle but was sorry she hadn't been there to comfort her mother.

The letter from Lulabelle was more troubling.

Darling Minta,

We are well and hope you are, too. Frank is still trying to secure enough capital to start his own store, but until then he continues with Mr. Haskel in his. I thought I was with child last month, but it turned out to be a false alarm. I do hope it happens soon.

I told you last time that I thought I'd seen Edmund lurking around. One of our neighbors told Frank he saw a man on our porch when we weren't home. He thought he might be going through our mail, but he couldn't be sure since the man had his back turned and was being secretive. I guess you were right. Well, he won't find you that way. Still, having him around so often makes me nervous. At least he has to go back to take care of his farm some of the time. Frank drove by there last time he was down that way on a buying trip for Mr. Haskel. He said things don't look nearly as well-kept up as they used to. Edmund must be spending a lot of his time, effort, and money looking for you instead of looking to his livelihood. I hope he'll get over that soon enough. You always said how proud he was of his farm.

Oh, yes—I told our minister about your situation (not where you are, of course), and he said a man had been asking around at all the local churches about missionaries in Oregon. Edmund must have suspicions about that letter. I asked Rev. Eldridge what he had told him, and he said he didn't know of any of the local Protestant churches sending missionaries there but that the Mormons probably did; or the Catholics might have a Mission there. Edmund must think you went to Oregon to be a missionary. I hope he goes chasing all over Oregon bothering the Mormons and Catholics, don't you? Maybe he'll get crossways of those Indians he was so worried about and get scalped.

The letter went on; Lulabelle was as wordy on paper as she was when she talked, but Minta stopped rereading there and crumpled the sheets, throwing them into her stove. She'd already penned an answer and didn't want any reminders of Edmund around. She didn't hope Edmund went to Oregon. He would have to travel too close to Colorado. And, if he were that determined to find her, he wouldn't stop with bothering the Catholics. She hoped Lulabelle was right about his "getting over it" but doubted she was. Minta knew him too well. He was like a bulldog with a bone when he wanted something his way.

Well, so was she. And she'd gotten her way. For now. Now she'd better go do her job.

February brought more snow but not enough to close school for more than the occasional day here and there. Still, a lot had piled up in the hills around them and, when the first thaw came in the middle of March, it hit heavy and fast. Minta had never seen so much water in little Halpern Creek. It was a chocolate brown, raging torrent with large logs, fence posts, and the occasional dead animal floating in it. Nearly every day she reemphasized the rule about staying inside the schoolyard fence. After school she walked the Woods, Archuleta, and Fredrickson children to the narrow, side-less bridge where one of their parents met them to walk them across. So far the bridge was holding, but the men checked it every day and, if it went, she'd lose half her students until the water went down and it could be repaired. At least the schoolhouse itself was built on high ground. Her cabin was lower but still out of harm's way to all but the worst flood. Fred told her it would take a heavy rainstorm on top of the snowmelt to cause that. So far, the days were clear and warm with no sign of rain.

The good weather had rekindled the kids' interest in softball, and they were determined to give Halpern School a run for its money at the end-of-school tournament. One rule for the contest was that all the students in each school had to be on their team and play in rotation. Halpern had the most big boys, but they also had the most little kids. So Rockytop's strategy was to teach the skills to their little kids so they would be better than Halpern's and, hopefully, make up for the fact that Rockytop only had two big boys. Michael was the pitcher, Angus the catcher and coach.

Every recess saw the kids practicing and refining their skills. The weakest link, of course, was little Gina, but Angus developed a strategy for her. He taught her to hold the bat on her shoulder (the only way she could) and crouch down, making a really small target area for the pitcher. Then she just stood there until she had four balls and walked to first base. They wanted Dale to do the same thing, but he insisted on swinging at everything that came his way. Once in a while he even connected, then ran around all the bases, regardless of where the ball ended up, Angus yelling at him in frustration. Oh, well—they were all learning and improving every day.

They had only one fairly beat-up bat and one much-patched softball, but what they lacked in equipment, they made up for in enthusiasm. They scratched bases in the dirt and redid them every time they got messed up, which was whenever anyone slid into base or if the baseman shuffled his feet. Minta made a rule that if the ball went outside the fence they had to call her to go get it. No one was to go outside the fence for any reason. So far they had obeyed that rule, and she kept her ears open for their calls during recess.

One morning Minta woke suddenly and early. A noise had awakened her, but what? Before drifting off to sleep the night before, she had heard coyotes calling, but she was sure that wasn't it now. This had been more high-pitched, like a scream almost. Well, she wouldn't be able to go back to sleep until she checked, so she lit her lantern and stepped outside the door of the cabin. Immediately, movement caught her eye, and she felt Blackie brush past her as the cat ran into the cabin and behind the stove. The movement took the shape of a coyote with something in its mouth.

It loped off, carrying whatever it was, as Minta stepped out the door. She walked to where it had been standing and held the lantern toward the ground. Blood. And gray fur. Then it hit her.

"Smokey! Oh, no—not Smokey!" Even as she said it, she knew it was true. The gray shape in the coyote's mouth could have been nothing else; the noise she heard, Smokey's death cry. No wonder Blackie had run in so terrified.

Back in the cabin, Minta coaxed Blackie out from behind the stove and sat on the floor with the cat in her lap, her tears dripping into the black fur. She knew it was silly to be so upset over a cat, but she couldn't help it. The cats had been her most faithful companions in this strange new place she called her home now. She'd been so happy to find them safe and well when she returned from the Archuletas', and she knew she had Angus to thank for that. Now, to have Smokey so cruelly and suddenly taken away was more than she thought she could bear.

She finally got herself under control, lit the stove, and put the coffee on to brew. There would be no going back to sleep; she might as well get something done. Her grandmother always said hard work would make her forget her troubles.

By the time she went over to open the school for the day, she'd already done a good day's work and was tired. But at least she wasn't thinking about Smokey. She decided to rest at her desk during morning recess instead of going out with the students. It was warm enough to open a window, so she could hear them if they needed her. She tried to grade papers, but her eyes kept blurring. Finally she put her head down on her arms and closed her eyes to rest them. She had almost drifted off to sleep when a sound outside alerted her.

"Oh, no!" Angus yelled. "Get it before it's too late."

Then Mary's voice, raised in alarm, "Robert, no!"

Minta got to the window in time to see Robert vault the fence and race headlong down the hill toward the creek and the escaping softball. Then she was out the door after him as fast as she could run. Mary had the gate open for her by the time she got there, and she ran after Robert, pulling her skirt up and leaping over rocks.

The ball was first in the procession to the river, bouncing its way in response to gravity's call. Robert was gaining on it but wasn't going to make it in time, Minta saw. "Robert, stop right now!" she yelled. Or tried to yell. She was out of breath. But her longer strides were gaining ground on Robert, and she reached him just as he reached the edge of the creek. They both watched the ball bounce inevitably into the raging water, surface once, and then disappear from sight forever.

Minta grabbed hold of the back of Robert's collar and pulled him back from the edge.

"Robert Haley, you scared me to death!"

"I wasn't going to fall in. I just wanted to save our ball."

"You broke the rule. Come with me." She kept hold of his collar as they turned and began the long march up the hill to the school. The rest of the students stood in silent dejection as they passed, the bat dangling useless now in Angus's grip.

Minta marched Robert into the schoolroom and, with the arm not holding his collar, opened the cupboard door and took out the so far unused ferule.

"What happened to the Three Strikes rule?" Robert asked. "That's only the first time I left the yard."

"When I made the rule, I said it wouldn't apply to things that were harmful or dangerous to you or anyone else. You don't get a second chance to hurt yourself."

"I told you. I wasn't going to fall in, I just . . ."

"Enough arguing. If you have anything in your back pockets, take it out. Now!"

Robert placed his pocket knife, a ball of string, and a smooth stone on a desk. Sighing in resignation, he bent over the desk, leaning on it with his arms.

Minta raised the ferule and brought it down with a sharp smack. She knew the open window would carry the sound to those gathered outside. Four more times and she was done. She went to her desk, placed the ferule there in plain sight, and rearranged her papers, giving Robert time to compose himself.

"Robert, after you've picked up your things from the desk, why don't you wash your hands and splash some cold water on your face? Then you can ring the bell for the end of recess."

The group that came in from recess was unaccustomedly quiet, slipping into their seats and industriously opening books and reading the instructions on the board. No one had the usual questions about what to do or why couldn't they do something else. Minta let them work that way, quietly on their own, until noon recess. They filed outside with their lard-buckets to eat lunch just as quietly. Minta stayed at her desk to eat hers, even though she'd rather be outside in the fresh air.

Their voices drifted in the window.

"Now we'll never beat Halpern," Michael said.

"It's Robert's fault. He hit that foul ball way over the fence," Angus said.

"Oh, Angus—a foul ball isn't anyone's fault. It just happened," Mary said. "Maybe if we all pooled our money, we could get a new ball the next time someone goes to Liberty."

"That might be a long time! We can't afford to lose our practice time," Michael said.

"What money?" Angus asked.

Minta wanted to run to her cabin and get some money from her meager stash to buy them a ball, but she wasn't sure that was the right thing to do. She'd have to think about how to handle this. The ball and bat were in the cloakroom when she first arrived. Maybe they were school property and the school board would replace . . . but no, that would mean telling Fred the whole story of what happened to the ball.

She realized the voices had changed tone, some angry and others alarmed. She walked toward the window as she heard Michael say, "Stop it, Angus! You're going to hurt somebody."

"Hold still and you won't get hurt," Angus said, as Minta looked out the window to see him throw his open pocket knife into the dirt at Michael's feet. Michael jumped back instinctively, and the blade stuck harmlessly in the dirt. Angus bent to pick it up.

"Angus, you know that playing mumbletypeg is against the rules," Mary said. "Please stop."

"'Please stop,'" Angus mimicked her. "We have to play something now that we don't have a ball, don't we? If you don't like it, go somewhere else."

"Well, I don't like it," Minta said out the window, "and I'm right here. Angus, come in right now." When he was standing defiantly before her, she held out her hand. "Give me the knife, Angus."

"I can't. I need this knife to do chores."

"You should have thought of that before you broke the rule. And, as you know, that's not just my rule. That's a state rule. Playing mumbletypeg is against the rule in all the schools."

"Okay. I won't do it any more, but please let me keep my knife. If I don't have it to do chores, Uncle Fred will want to know why and . . ."

"All right. You may keep your knife, this time. If I ever see it used inappropriately again on school property, I *will* take it and keep it until the end of the school year. Is that clear?"

"Yes, ma'am. Can I go now?"

"May you go now. No. We're not done here. As I told Robert, there are no three strikes for breaking rules that can hurt someone. Take . . ."

"I didn't hurt anyone."

"I said can hurt someone. You didn't, but you could have. Now, if you have anything else in your back pockets, take it out."

Angus's eyes widened. "You aren't going to whip me."

"Yes, I am."

"You can't. I'm bigger . . . ." He measured her with his eyes. She still had a couple inches on him. "We'll, I'm stronger than you."

"Yes, I'm sure you are, but that has nothing to do with it. You can cooperate with me now, or we can go to Fred after school and tell him you refused to cooperate. Which is it to be?"

Minta put all her considerable strength into the swats from the ferule this time, and she didn't stop with five. After the eighth one, she said, "Okay. Stand up. Look at me. I will not allow you or Robert or any of the other kids to hurt themselves or anyone else in my school. I will do whatever it takes to keep you all safe. Do you understand?"

He kept his head down and nodded. Finally, he looked up, and his dark eyes were guarded and unreadable. At least they weren't defiant as before. She was worried she'd been a little excessive, but, considering his age and size, she wanted to make an impression he wouldn't soon forget.

After lunch recess was over, Minta decided she couldn't stand a whole afternoon of strained silence like the morning had been. She changed the routine and announced she was going to read another chapter in *The Adventures of Tom Sawyer* to them. The younger students clapped their hands in anticipation, since they had left Becky lost in the cave that morning and were anxious to find out what happened. After she finished the chapter, Minta just kept reading. It was all she had the energy left to do. They finished the book in time for afternoon recess, but she didn't want to risk what new catastrophe it might bring, so she told them they could finish up their board work and get out a little early in lieu of recess. They were all in favor of that plan and went back to work willingly.

It was Judith and Michael's turn to help after school. The rest of the combined Haley clan waited for them outside, leaning on the fence in the shade, not used to the hot sun yet. Minta returned from walking the other-side-of-the-river kids to the bridge about the time Judy and Michael finished sweeping and straightening the schoolroom. After Michael came in from cleaning the erasers, Minta told Judy to go tell everyone else to come in for a minute. They lined up, looking at her expectantly.

"About what happened today," she began.

"I know, I know," Robert said. "I'm going to be in more trouble at home."

"Not half as much as Angus is," Michael said. "At least you were trying to do something good, not something bad."

"Breaking the rules is always bad," Minta said. "What I'm trying to say is that what happened today is between Robert and me and Angus and me. If they want to bring it up at home, they can. The rest of you don't need to be mentioning it."

"You mean you're not going to tell on us?" Robert asked.

"I don't plan to bring the subject up," Minta said. "Of course, if your parents ever ask me a direct question, I won't lie to them."

"That's all well and good," Angus said. "But I'll bet Dale and Judy can't keep their mouths shut."

"We can, too," Dale said angrily. "Can't we, Judy?"

Judy frowned. "Huh?"

"I'll explain it to her on the way home," Mary said. "Let's go."

They filed out the door, Dale last. He turned at the doorway and ran back in to Minta, throwing his arms around her knees, hugging the only part of her he could reach.

"What's that for, Dale?" Minta asked.

"I hope you don't neva whip me," he said.

"I hope I don't ever need to, Dale. Now hurry up and catch up with the others. I don't want you walking home alone."

She watched as he caught up with Michael and Angus, wiggling in-between them and reaching up for their hands. They took his in theirs and kept walking.

CHAPTER SIXTEEN

Games

༄ঞ৵

Thursday, April 8, 1920—*Our warm March turned into a cold, windy April. Mornings are usually nice once the chill gets sunned off, but afternoons are nearly always windy. Still, the kids are determined to keep practicing softball. I made a ball, of sorts. I remembered how Mother used to use strips of cotton rags to make rugs. She'd sew the strips together end to end and roll them into a tight ball before braiding them into a rug. I made such a ball out of some cleaning rags and then made a sack for it out of burlap and sewed it tightly all around. It's about the size, shape, and weight of a softball, but it doesn't really work right when you hit it with the bat. It doesn't go as far or as straight as a real ball and needs to be mended after every few hits. But we've devised several practice games that it does work for: throwing and catching, of course, and we invented a game called "Running the Bases Tag." Kids try to steal bases while others throw the ball to each other and try to tag them out. Michael also throws pinecones to the kids to try to hit with the bat to improve their batting skills. And he practices pitching by throwing my poor ball into a target area. Angus calls the strikes and balls. All in all, we're making do.*

I think the schoolwork is going as well as can be expected, too. There are the usual problems with Angus and grammar, and with several of the others and math. The first graders have all started to read reasonably well, except little Gina. Honor continues to be a big help on Wednesdays. I do hope she can go on to high school. She could be a good teacher someday.

Teresa told me yesterday that Jaime rolled over on his own and was smiling and laughing now. He's still awfully small and frail looking, but it looks like he'll make it.

And Honor told me her mother is expecting again. So Dale won't be the baby of the Haley family any more. Oh dear, I'm so caught up in the doings of all the people here, I hardly remember I had another life not too long ago. Well, that's what I wanted. I guess.

Later that night, Minta's eyes flew open at a familiar sound—one that haunted her nightmares. Not again! Where was Blackie? She jumped out of bed, calling the cat's name. At first, after Smokey's death, she had kept Blackie in at night. But the poor cat would cry to get out, scratching at the carpetbag in front of the hole until Minta couldn't stand it and would let her out. Finally, she just decided to let the cat come and go at will and hope for the best. Blackie had always been more cautious than Smokey.

The cry came again, louder and angry sounding. At least the cat was still alive. Minta raced out of the cabin door barefoot and in her nightgown, thankful that there was a full moon so she didn't need to stop to light the lantern. She thought the sound had come from the creek side of the cabin. Since she had no weapon, she grabbed the broom from beside the door on her way out.

Minta stopped a few yards from the cabin and looked around. Then she heard the sound again—snarling cat voices, two of them, it sounded like. Her eyes followed the sound and she saw Blackie with another, bigger cat. It must be that big Tom of Valoris'. They were fighting—no—not fighting. Minta stopped in her tracks, holding the broom uncertainly. Should she interfere, try to chase Tom away with the broom? Blackie yowled again, but she wasn't trying to get away. Minta hoped the male cat wasn't hurting Blackie. If Minta didn't interfere, maybe there would be kittens to play with soon. It would be fun to watch them chase each other all over the cabin as Blackie and Smokey had done. Minta lowered her broom and walked gingerly back into the cabin, noticing the pain from the rocks and sticks on the soles of her bare feet that she hadn't felt on her flight out.

She crawled back into bed and pulled the covers up, but she couldn't go back to sleep. Did Blackie like what the male cat was doing to her? Claudia apparently liked doing what one had to do to conceive a child. Was there some other way besides the violent way Edmund had gone about it? Surely, if his way were the only way, there would be many fewer children in the world. And more broken marriages. She hadn't thought about it before, but Edmund was mean in so many other ways, why not in that one as well? If she were ever free to marry again, maybe that part of it wouldn't be so bad. But she couldn't let herself think about that. To do so would be to wish another human being dead, another sin to add to her list of transgressions.

She tried to imagine what being married to someone other than Edmund might be like. She thought of Silas's words, of his promise that he would never hurt her and wouldn't do anything she didn't want him to. But he was a man, and men had "needs," according to Edmund, that couldn't be denied. But she was back to Edmund, and thoughts of marrying anyone else were just wistful thinking. She'd never be free to marry again. At least not until she was so old that conceiving children wouldn't be an option.

In spite of her troubling thoughts, she did go back to sleep. She dreamed Blackie had six kittens and they all looked like Haley children. Then Silas came and took her on his horse to someplace far away where the grass was green and soft. He laid her down in the grass and took off all her clothes, gently, not ripping off buttons and tearing as Edmund often did. Silas had a white Santa beard on and it tickled her naked flesh as he bent over her. His horse made a sound like an angry cat; then she realized that the beard was all Silas had on, and she was suddenly frightened. She woke up flushed and panting, tangled in the sheets but with an unfamiliar damp warmth in her woman's place. She wished the dream had continued.

As if her nighttime visions had conjured him up, Silas presented himself at the school door shortly before afternoon recess. Minta felt her face flush when she saw him, remembering her dream of the night before.

"Sorry to interrupt, ma'am," he said.

The pupils all turned in their seats to see who had come in and what had made their teacher go suddenly pale, then pink. Gertie giggled and whispered something to Florence, who looked at Minta and broke out laughing.

"Girls!" Minta snapped. "That's enough!" Then she turned to their visitor. "What did you want, Silas?" she asked, rather too sharply.

"Well, I brought something. Something for the school, I mean. Is it okay if I bring it in?" He was grinning like a kid on Christmas morning.

"I guess so. What is it?" she asked, as the students all put down their work and turned to see what Silas would bring in.

He went back out into the cloakroom and returned, holding a brand new bat in one hand and tossing a new softball up in the air and catching it with the other. The room erupted into shouts of joy and clapping hands.

"Silas, we can't accept those. You can't afford . . ."

"Oh, I didn't buy them. They're from Old Ma . . . Mr. Rickerts. He heard about what happened to your ball, and he said he wanted to do something for the school in thanks for all the potlucks and school programs he's enjoyed over the years. Besides, he says he's sick of Halpern always winning the tournament, and he'll do anything he can to 'hep somebody show them polecats up, by grannies,'" he imitated Rickerts' rough, gravelly voice.

Minta laughed. "Well, I can't promise him that. But I will promise we'll give it our best shot, won't we boys and girls?"

They all shouted agreement, and Dale jumped up out of his seat. "Can we go pwacktice wight now, Miss Mayfield? It's 'most time for wecess. Please, please?" Other voices were raised in agreement, the formerly dull school day having turned electric with excitement.

Minta lifted the watch pin on her bodice so she could see the time. "We have fifteen more minutes until recess. I'll cut that down to ten if you all get back to work and show me how much you can get done in those ten minutes." They bent to their tasks, even Dale concentrating on the spelling list he was copying.

Silas was still standing uncertainly in the back of the room. Minta walked back to him and took the ball and bat from him. "Was there something else, Silas? Oh, thank you! And please thank Mr. Rickerts for us. I'll have the students write a proper thank-you note to him after recess and send it with you, too. But how did he know? About the ball being lost, I mean?"

"Oh, it's all over the valley. Everyone knows—even the Halpern bunch. He couldn't stand their gloating. He said he heard 'that confounded, highfalutin' Ben Griffith' saying your kids were such bad hitters they couldn't tell center creek from center field."

"I guess I shouldn't be surprised. Not many secrets around here," she said. Except mine, she thought. Both Claudia and Sophie tried to get her to talk about her past life, but she always put them off by changing the subject. She knew there was speculation about where she came from and why.

"Yes, there is something else," Silas said. "If it's okay, I'll wait outside and discuss it with you after school." Minta was apprehensive about what he wanted, but she couldn't very well tell him to go away after he brought the gifts to them.

When she finally dismissed the students for recess, they passed the new bat and ball from hand to hand, admiring the newness, feeling the smooth wood, and smelling the new-ball smell.

"It seems a shame to use them and get them all scratched and dirty," Mary said.

"What a dumb-girl thing to say," Angus said with disgust. "What's the point of having them, then?"

"Angus, what have I said about name calling?" Minta said.

"Sorry, Mary," he apologized. "But I'm worried. The stream is still pretty high. What if this ball goes down there, too? You can whip me all you want, ma'am. I'm going to try to save it if it does. We're not losing this ball!"

Silas, who had been sitting on the step, stood up. "I have an idea about that," he said. "Minta, I mean, Miss Mayfield can—I mean may—I show you something?"

She smiled at his awkward attempts at correct grammar as he led them all out of the school and to the back of the schoolyard. He pointed to the meadow behind the back fence. "I know it's outside the fence, but what if you made the softball field back there? It's flat enough, and there's no way a ball could get to the stream from there."

"Yeah," Michael said. "You could tell us where we couldn't go, ma'am, like up Rockytop Hill on that side or past that grove of trees over there. We'll stay inside whatever boundaries you say, even if there's not a fence." The others nodded their agreement, their faces alight with hopeful expectation—Silas's too. She couldn't deny any of them.

So that's what they did. The children went happily to work removing rocks from the playing field and scratching out bases. Silas joined them, offering advice, stepping out distances from base to base with his long stride, and then staying on to act as umpire for their first practice session. Minta leaned on the fence behind him, watching the way his muscles rippled beneath his shirt when he'd fling his arm out to yell "strike" or "ball." He was such a good man. She couldn't imagine Edmund ever bringing a ball and bat as gifts for a school and then staying to play with the kids. He'd be more likely to use the bat on the students and throw the ball into the creek the first time something made him mad.

Silas was intent on the game, but once in a while he'd glance over his shoulder to see if she was still there, obviously very aware of her. She felt that warmth again, like after her dream, and decided it was time to go back to work. She turned and walked reluctantly back to her desk and the pile of papers waiting for her there.

After all the kids had gone home after school, Silas was still waiting for her.

"Oh, I forgot," she said. "You said there was something else you wanted to talk about."

"Yes. Maybe we could discuss it in your cabin over a cup of coffee or something? Don't worry," he said quickly, seeing her look of dismay. "I don't have designs on your virtue. I'd just rather talk there than in a schoolroom, if you don't mind."

"Of course." Minta had noticed that many of the adults, especially the men, seemed to feel awkward and out of place in the schoolroom. She supposed it had to do with their memories of school, or of school teachers.

Once they were settled at her table with cups of reheated breakfast coffee and her last two cookies, she looked at Silas expectantly.

"I don't know quite how to explain all this, so I guess I'll just light right in. Old Man Rickerts and I went to town for more than that bat and ball," he began. "All he told me was he wanted to go talk to the lawyer. So I took him in and, when we got there, he said, 'Silas, how much money you got in your pitiful pocket?' I pulled out a dollar and fifty-three cents, and he said, 'Gimme a buck fifty.' So I did. Then he turned to the lawyer and said, 'I'm selling my place to this boy here, for one dollar and fifty cents. Don't want to run him clean out of money, so I'm letting him keep the three cents. Draw up the papers.'"

"Oh, my," Minta said. "Claudia says Rickerts' is the best place in the whole valley."

"Yep. He was the first homesteader in here after they opened it up, so he got the place with the spring and the best grass."

"So, what happened? What did you do?"

"Well, I said I couldn't take his place like that. What would he do? So he said there was strings attached. I asked what, and he said he wanted to keep living there until he died. He said if he got too ornery to take care of I should just take him out and shoot him—but, of course, I said I'd never do that. He said this winter when he had the pneumonia so bad and thought he was going to die, he wondered what would happen to his place. He doesn't have any family to leave it to. And he sure doesn't want the government, or as he says, 'gol-durned gummit,' to get it."

"I remember. You nursed him through that illness, didn't you?"

"Yeah. That's what he said made him think of it. That I should have the place in exchange for taking care of him in his old age."

"So, is it all done?"

"Yep, life done dealt me a new hand. You're looking at a landowner. I never thought I'd have my own place. Figured I'd be working for other people my whole life."

"That's wonderful, Silas. You deserve it. I'm happy for you."

"You know what this means, don't you?" Silas cupped her chin in his hand, forcing her to look into his eyes.

She tried to keep her gaze steady and neutral. "Yes, it means you've got a lot of work to do and so do I, so we'd better call it a day." She leaned back out of his grasp and rose, hoping he'd take the hint and leave.

He stayed put. "It means I've got a place to call my own. A place I could raise a family. I know before, when I was just some drifter, I wasn't a very good catch—but now I've got something to offer a woman."

"Yes, you do, Silas. I hope you find her." Minta turned to look out the window so he wouldn't see her face.

"I already have." He came and stood behind her and gently tried to turn her head, his hand on her chin again.

"Silas, please," Minta walked to the door and opened it, desperate to get rid of him before her tears started. "I told you, I'm not interested."

"And I told you, I don't take no for an answer without a fight. Is it because of that Edmund feller, whoever he is?"

"Yes. It's because of Edmund. You promised you wouldn't bring him up again. Now please leave me alone."

Silas reached for her shoulder. She shrugged away. "I could make you forget him," he said. "Whatever happened, if he left you for another woman, or broke your heart, or whatever he did to make you so upset . . ."

"Leave, Silas—now!" Minta said, pushing him toward the door, her hands hot against his shoulder blades, wanting to get rid of him and at the same time wishing she could keep her hands against his strong body forever. She slammed the door behind him and leaned against it, her tears staining the wood as she heard his horse's hoofbeats fade into the distance.

CHAPTER SEVENTEEN
Pride Goeth Before a Fall

ᴄ⟋ꞁ⟍ꜱ

Monday, May 3, 1920—*Sad news. Florence and Wendell won't be in my school next year. Luke says he's tired of trying to scratch a living out of this valley and has gotten a job at the lumberyard in Durango. They'll be moving as soon as school is out. Fred's going to lease their place with the option to buy it, eventually. I'm sorry to lose the kids, but Luke hasn't been happy here since his wife died. The silver lining in the whole thing is that Honor will be able to stay with them and go to high school. She'll keep house and help with the kids in exchange for her room and board.*

I realize I'm being presumptuous saying they won't be in MY school, since no one has asked me to teach here again next year. I'm assuming they will ask me, but I won't feel safe for another year until I sign that piece of paper again. I wonder if I should ask Fred or Matthew about it?

I can't believe there is only a month of school left! We have so much yet to do, so much more I want to teach them. Is it ever enough time, I wonder? I look back to the beginning, and I can't believe how much I've learned here—not just about teaching, but about life. Much more than the students have, I'm sure. I can see mistakes I made at first and want so much to try again to do it better next year, although I am proud of what I've done here this year. Well, I'll just have to do what I can in the time left and let tomorrow worry about tomorrow, as Grandmother would say.

"Not another math test," Gunny groaned when Minta announced it. "We just had one last week."

"Yes," Minta said. "And you didn't do very well on it, as I recall. Now you get another chance to study and do better. So, get busy."

"It's like this every year," Michael sighed. "As soon as the end of school gets close, the teacher doubles our work."

"I haven't doubled your work. But you all do have quite a bit you need to finish up before June first."

"June first! The all-school picnic! The day we beat Halpern!" Robert shouted. "I can't wait. We're going to pluck their chickens."

"Pride goeth before a fall," Mary said, just as Minta was opening her mouth to do so.

"All of you, back to work!" Minta ordered. She sighed: It was getting harder and harder to keep them focused on work as the May flowers pushed up out of the ground and began to bloom. And the May fields (she smiled) turned green. Was it only a year ago that she had adopted her new name after the May fields of Indiana? Well, these outside her windows were just as beautiful, if not as well groomed. There she was—daydreaming, just like the students.

She forced her attention back to the lesson plans she was writing on the pad on her desk. The first week of May. Time really was getting short.

After school Fred pulled up in his wagon, obviously on his way back from town. His children were excited to get an unaccustomed ride home. Minta expected him to drive off as soon as the children piled into the wagon, but instead, he told them to stay put and came into the school. Oh, good. Maybe he had brought her contract for next year. She walked to the back to meet him.

"There's an emergency school meeting tonight, Minta, at seven," he said. "You might want to put the school in order. I expect pretty much everyone will be here."

"Emergency? What emergency?"

"I can't tell you that. I don't even know. Matthew just told me in town to have everyone here, that it was important. Oh, yes, and that he'd be bringing a couple people."

"Who?"

"I told you. I don't know any more about it than you do. But I've never seen Matthew so grave. It must be something pretty serious."

Minta's plan to take a walk downstream to her favorite grove of cottonwoods was quickly abandoned. In order to have a large meeting in here, she'd have to put away many of the books and supplies she'd just gotten out for tomorrow's lessons. She should probably erase at least one of the boards she'd prepared for tomorrow, too, in case they needed it for the meeting, whatever it was about.

She couldn't imagine what would cause Matthew to call an emergency meeting. Had the school district run out of funds? Were they going to close her school next year? Oh, please, God, don't let it be that. She prayed as she worked.

After a quick snack for supper, Minta put on her best outfit—the one she wore to church. She wasn't sure why; she normally wouldn't wear it to school or to a meeting. It just seemed fitting. She locked Blackie in the cabin by rolling a large rock in front of the hole from the outside. Since losing Smokey, Blackie often followed Minta around for companionship. The cat was used to wandering in and out of the schoolhouse at will, but there might be people there tonight who wouldn't appreciate its presence.

Nearly everyone had gathered by seven, and they waited impatiently for Matthew and whoever he was bringing to come. Fred announced that Matthew had said it wasn't a meeting for children, so they sent them to the teacherage under Honor's care. The two babies stayed at the meeting with their mothers, along with little Joseph Valori, who was never left with anyone other than his parents. On the children's way out, Minta handed Honor some books to read to them.

Shortly after they left, Angus slipped quietly back in and stood near the cloakroom door. Minta saw Fred notice him and frown, but before he had a chance to say anything, someone looking out the window said, "Here they come. That's Matthew's buggy. I believe that's the sheriff riding alongside, and Matthew and somebody else are in the buggy. Can't tell who yet."

They all moved away from the windows as the men outside left the buggy and made their way through a schoolyard full of conveyances to come inside.

Minta was standing behind her desk and recognized the sheriff, Moses Upton, whom she'd met in Liberty over Christmas break. The stranger was a tall man with a large hat on. His back was to her as he took it off and turned around. Minta felt her heart skip a beat as she gripped the edge of the desk with her fingers. Her knees buckled and she fell into her chair with a gasp. "Edmund!"

His face arranged itself into what passed for a smile with him and said, "Yes, Ella. I've found you at last."

But how? Minta wanted to scream. How had he found her?

The room had fallen into sudden silence as everyone looked from Minta to Edmund, trying to figure out what was going on. Time seemed to stop for Minta. She was vaguely aware of rustling and hushed whispers of "Ella?" and scraping chairs, but all she could see, looming larger than life, was Edmund.

In the silence, the sheriff and Matthew strode to the front of the room. Matthew put his hand firmly on Minta's shoulder and said, "Minta, this man has made some accusations against you. I thought you should have a chance to tell your side of the story, too. I convinced the sheriff to go along with my plan, as long as you promise not to try to leave until we have this all sorted out. I asked everyone else to come so they can hear it all firsthand, instead of secondhand. Then they can make up their minds about what they want to do about the rest of the school year."

Minta looked up in a fog. If it were possible, she would run out the door and keep running until she dropped from exhaustion. But that was impossible. There were too many people between her and the door—including Edmund, still standing next to the exit. She couldn't leave. She'd have to stay and face whatever happened. From deep inside herself, she drew up the will not to cry. Whatever happened, she would not cry in this room in front of these people. At least all the lying was over. She felt her bottom lip in the grip of her teeth.

The sheriff cleared his throat. "Why don't you start, Mr. Skraggs?" he said to Edmund. "Then we'll let the little lady say her piece."

Edmund made his way to the front of the room and stood looking down at Minta, who refused to make eye contact with him. "There's not much to say," he said. "That's not Minta or whatever she's calling herself now. That's my wife. All I want is for her to come home with me." He sounded very reasonable. Minta knew how well he could play one part for the world to see and another very different one at home.

"Well, Miss Mayfield," the sheriff said. "Is that true? Is this man your husband?"

She took a deep breath and found her voice. "We were married, yes."

"Were? You're not now?" Matthew asked.

"Yes, I suppose we still are, legally," she said. "But I will not go back with him." She turned her attention from the men in front and looked at the people. "I will understand if you don't want me as your teacher any more, but I will not go back."

"Now, Ella, be reasonable. You don't want all these people to hear about our marital problems, do you? Let's just let bygones be bygones and go home." Edmund tried to maneuver closer to Minta, but the other two men were in the way.

"Is there a reason you don't want to go back, Minta?" Claudia asked from the front row.

Minta's eyes found Claudia's, so good and kind. "I don't want to go back because he will hurt me," she said.

"Do you mean physically hurt you?" Claudia asked, frowning.

Minta nodded. It was humiliating to have to tell what Edmund did to her in front of all these people, but if she had to, she would.

"He hits me. Sometimes with his fists, sometimes with objects. And he likes to . . ."

Edmund interrupted her. "See? I told you she'd say something of the sort." He turned to the sheriff. "She hasn't been right since she fell off that horse last year. She kept insisting that I was the one who caused her injuries, even though I wasn't even with her. I've found a doctor back East to take her to—you know, a head doctor. I think he can help her. It's obvious she isn't right. Look at what she did: changing her name, lying to all you good people. I'll bet you've noticed some odd behaviors since she's been here."

"Well, if you call being the best teacher we've ever had in this valley 'odd behavior,' then I guess we have," Hannah said. "And I don't think you can make her go back against her will, can he, Sheriff? If there's even a little bit of truth to what she said, she shouldn't be made to go back."

"Well, no, I guess not. No law says a woman has to live with her husband," the sheriff answered.

"What about the law against adultery?" Edmund demanded. "I'll bet she's been seeing other men since she's been here, hasn't she?"

Minta became aware of a commotion in back as Silas stepped forward, his face red and angry. "No, she hasn't," he said. "I mean, she tried real hard not to see men, but we—some of us—wouldn't leave her alone. But she hasn't committed adultery."

Edmund looked down his nose at Silas. "You know that for a fact, do you, cowboy?"

Silas clenched his fists, but just said, "Yes, I do. And I know for a fact she's afraid of some mangy devil named Edmund. That'd be you, now, wouldn't it?"

The sheriff stepped between them. "Let's all remain calm here. Why don't you go sit back down, Silas?" He did, reluctantly.

Minta stood up and looked from face to face in the crowd—all the people she'd come to know and love. Even Angus, standing in back, his eyes on his boots. What was he thinking of her? What were they all?

"I want to tell all of you how sorry I am," she said. "Not sorry I came here. I'll never be sorry I did that. I've loved it here. But sorry I lied to you. I thought it was the only thing I could do at the time. I didn't know how else to escape from a man who would eventually have killed me, one way or another. He still will, if you don't help me now . . ."

"Oh, for heaven's sake," Edmund exploded. "Are you going to let her carry on like this? I've explained the situation to you."

"Yes, you have," Matthew said. "And the sheriff explained to you that you can't take her with you if she doesn't want to go. So I suggest you go back where you came from, and we'll deal with our teacher issues on our own."

Edmund turned to the sheriff. "I want this woman arrested, Sheriff," he said.

"On what grounds? I don't see a case for adultery."

"Theft. She stole a good horse, my best buggy and all its tack, and several other items from me when she left. She needs to be returned to Indiana to face those charges."

"Is that true, Miss . . . er . . . Missus? Did you do that?" the Sheriff asked.

"Well, yes. I mean, I had to take them to get away and then sell them to get money for the train. He never allowed me to have any money of my own—not even my inheritance from my grandmother that I brought to the marriage."

Claudia stood up and walked over to where Fred was leaning on the blackboard. She turned and confronted Edmund. "How many horses did you own? And was that buggy your only vehicle?"

"I have four horses, besides that one, and two wagons, and various other pieces of farm equipment. So what?"

"If you were married to her, as you keep insisting, then half of what you own should belong to her. It sounds to me like she didn't even take her half." Claudia turned to Fred. "Isn't that right, Fred? As your wife, I'm entitled to half of all you own, aren't I?"

Fred smiled down at his wife and took her by the shoulders. "No, dear," he said, causing an audible gasp to pass through the room. "As my wife, you're entitled to *all* I own," he finished. Claudia smiled and leaned against him.

In spite of her resolve, Minta felt tears spring to her eyes. Of all the men in the world, why had she ended up with Edmund? And how had Edmund ended up here? There was only one way. She turned to the sheriff. "Is there some way you can quickly contact some people in Indiana for me? Telegraph or something? The only way Edmund could have found me here is through my cousin and her husband. And they would never willingly tell him."

Her eyes widened as she turned to look fully at Edmund for the first time. "Oh, Edmund—what did you do to Lulabelle?" The corners of his mouth turned up as he looked at her, his eyes black as coal dust. She knew that look. Whatever he'd done to Lulabelle, he'd enjoyed doing.

She turned back toward the sheriff. "He must have hurt them some way. I must find out if they're all right."

"Okay," the sheriff said. "Here's what we'll do. I'll contact the law in Indiana and find out if there's a warrant out on you for theft. I'll also have them check on your relatives, if you give me their names and addresses. That might take a couple days. We'll meet back here night after tomorrow night. At that time, if either of you people needs to be arrested, I'll do it. In the meantime, I'm placing you in the custody of Fred Haley, and Mr. Skraggs will come back to town with me."

Edmund reluctantly left with the sheriff and Matthew Post. Going out the cloakroom door, he suddenly tripped and nearly fell, managing to catch himself awkwardly on the door jam. He stopped and glared at Angus, who was innocently and intently looking at his fingernails as he slid his scuffed boot back. Realizing people were watching him, Edmund followed the other two men out the door.

Fred stepped up to the desk and faced the crowd. "I guess school is canceled until further notice. See you all in two nights. Be thinking what you want done about all this. And about next school year. We'll decide when we get back together."

As people trickled out the door, most avoided looking at Minta. Fred turned to her. "Can I trust you to stay in your cabin, or do you need to come home with us?"

"Oh, for heaven's sake, Fred," Claudia said before Minta had to answer. "Of course she can stay in her own cabin. Unless you'd rather come with us? Minta?"

"No, thank you. I want to be alone."

Finally, Minta was sitting alone at her kitchen table. "I want to be alone" were the last words she'd spoken to anyone. And she was. Alone. Really alone. In spite of the love and support she'd felt from Silas, Claudia, and a few others, it was her problem to deal with—alone. Again. She opened her diary.

CHAPTER EIGHTEEN

Refuge

✧❦✧

Monday evening, May 3, 1920—*I have decided what to do. I sat here at this table for an hour after the meeting trying to decide, and it finally became clear to me. Edmund could not have found me without hurting Lulabelle and Frank in some way. He knows the sheriff will find that out, so he can't wait around for the meeting in two days. Going back to town with the sheriff was only a ruse. At the first opportunity he will come for me, probably tonight. I can't stay here, and I can't go to Haleys' and put all of them in danger.*

I will pack my two bags with what I can carry. Blackie will follow me, so I will go by Valoris' and shut her up in an outbuilding. They will find her soon and take care of her and her soon-to-come kittens. Then I must leave the road. Edmund will come by the road. But there is no moon tonight, and I might lose my way. I will find a place to hide until morning, well away from the houses. Then I will make my way cross country to the reservation. I don't know how the Indians will react to a strange woman in their midst, but I'd rather take my chances with them than with Edmund. Maybe I can teach at a reservation school. At any rate, he won't look for me there. Like most bullies, he's afraid of anyone who might be stronger than he is, and I know he fears the Indians.

I am writing this down in case I don't make it. I will keep it with me to the end. If Edmund finds me or I succumb to the elements before I find help, I want someone to know what happened. I will carry what water I can with me. I know it's hard to find once I leave the area drained by the Liberty River. The names and addresses of my relatives are in the back cover of this volume. Please let them know what happened to me and how sorry I am for all the pain I have caused them.

Now I will spend a few minutes with my Bible and in prayer. Then I will pack and go. Thank you, diary, for your faithful companionship. This may well be my last entry.

Minta opened her Bible to Psalms. She usually found the verses soothing, but 27:12 jolted her as she read:

> *Deliver me not over unto the will of mine enemies: for false witnesses are risen up against me, and such as breathe out cruelty.*

She couldn't help but think of Edmund. If anyone breathed out cruelty, he did. Quickly she turned to Psalm 34, since she knew its message would be more comforting. It seemed to confirm her flight from Edmund when it said,

> *Depart from evil and do good; seek peace, and pursue it.*

She had tried to depart from his evil and do good. She had sought peace and now she must continue to pursue it, wherever her flight would take her.

She skipped ahead in Psalms and read without comprehending, just letting the words flow, calming her cluttered brain. Suddenly a phrase jumped out at her, and she stopped and started over with Psalm 61:

> *Hear my cry, O God, attend unto my prayer.*
>
> *From the end of the earth will I cry unto thee, when my heart is overwhelmed: lead me to the rock that is higher than I.*
>
> *For thou hast been a shelter for me, and a strong tower from the enemy.*

Minta looked up through the black window toward Rockytop, even though it was too dark to see it. "The rock that is higher than I," she thought. Rockytop? "From the end of the earth I cry to thee"—this valley feels likes the end of the earth. God led me here to that rock that is higher than I, a shelter and a strong tower from the enemy. Edmund, my enemy. Once, as a small child watching her grandmother do her daily Bible reading and prayer, Minta had asked, "Grandmother, you talk to God all the time. Does He talk to you?"

"Oh, yes he does, Ella," she'd answered. "God talks to me through the scriptures." She held up her Bible for the little girl to see. "He'll talk to you someday, too, dear."

Dear God, are you telling me to go to Rockytop? Minta thought. It sure sounds like it. Dare I stay so close to the cabin? I could watch for Edmund from there. If he comes to the cabin and finds me and my things gone, he will assume I have fled and go look elsewhere. And even if he does sense my presence somehow and attempts to climb Rockytop, I can always throw myself over the other side. But what about the snakes? Do they come out at night? She didn't know. But she had meant what she had told Lulabelle about preferring to face snakes than Edmund.

Feeling as if she were being led, Minta finished packing and picked up her two suitcases. She was taking only what she came with, plus two additions: the scarf Honor had made her, carefully wrapped around the bird crafted by Michael and Angus. She blew out the lantern and started toward the door, when she heard hoofbeats coming quickly toward the cabin. She had delayed too long! Frantically she felt around the room for a weapon and picked up the iron poker for the fire. Holding it in both hands, she faced the door as someone knocked on it.

Hardly daring to breathe, she held her ground. It wasn't like Edmund to knock. He must not be sure this was the right cabin. Maybe if she didn't answer and no light showed inside, he would go away. No such luck. The door opened, and she tensed her muscles, ready to strike out.

"Whoa, steady now," Silas said, as she stepped toward him, the poker raised. "It's me, Silas. I can barely see you. It sure is dark tonight."

She lowered the poker. "Oh, Silas. You scared me. Again."

"I'm sorry. I got all the way home, and then I decided you shouldn't be alone tonight."

"You know Edmund will come, too, then?"

"No, not that. Do you think he will? I thought he went back to town with the sheriff. I mean, you shouldn't be alone—with your thoughts, after all that was said at the meeting. Why are your suitcases packed?"

"I'm leaving. I know Edmund will come for me."

"I'll stay with you. I'll protect you. In fact, I'd like nothing better than to wipe that smug look off his . . ."

"No. I can't put anyone else in danger. The damage I've already caused is bad enough." She picked up her suitcases and started for the door.

"But, where are you going?"

"Up Rockytop, for now. I'm going to hide up there until I'm sure Edmund is gone. Then I'll go—somewhere. It's clear I can't stay here, anyway."

"Why not? At the meeting, it kinda sounded like at least some of the people wanted you to stay."

"Edmund knows where I am and, besides, once they have a chance to think about what I've done, no one will want me here now. I can't keep teaching their children. I've been proven a thief and a liar. I deceived them when they hired me; I deceived you. It's unforgivable. Now, get out of my way. Edmund could be here any time."

Silas relit the lantern and walked over to the bed and began tearing it apart.

"What are you doing?" she asked, setting down the suitcases.

"Making a bedroll. It's going to be cold on Rockytop tonight."

"I can't take any more. I've got all I can carry."

"I'm coming with you," Silas said firmly. "And, by the way, *I* forgive you. I'm sure most others will, too."

She felt she should continue arguing with him, but she didn't really want to. The thought of a night alone on Rockytop was only slightly less repugnant than the thought of waiting for Edmund to come. But she would be putting Silas in danger. A phrase from the verse in Psalms jumped unbidden into her head: "a strong tower." Silas Tower? She'd never forgive herself if something happened to him.

"Silas, I can't let you . . ."

"You aren't *letting* me. I make my own decisions. Now, are we going to stand here arguing until he comes, or make our getaway?"

They unsaddled his horse, led it to the stream, then turned it loose to graze. It would find a place to bed down for the night. They couldn't have it hanging around at the base of Rockytop as a clue to their presence. Fortunately, he'd made Yowler stay home with Rickerts tonight.

Silas carried her large case in one hand, the bedroll under his arm, and the lantern in the other hand. She carried the small case and a squirming Blackie. When they got to the rocks, Silas used the lantern to find good footing as they made their way up through the cleft she'd found the day she climbed Rockytop. They found a sheltered area that would allow them a view of the valley but not let them be seen from below once the lantern was extinguished.

"I'm worried about snakes," Minta said. "Do they come out at night?"

"Not this time of year. It's still too cold. Besides, the farmers and ranchers have been killing every one they see for years, especially after Richard Haley died. There aren't that many left. And those that are stay away from people if they can help it. You don't see one very often anymore, except off away from civilization. I think they keep up the stories about snakes on Rockytop to keep the kids from playing up here."

He spread the bedroll out in a patch of dirt between two large boulders, and they settled themselves to a night of waiting. A cool breeze was blowing, but down between the boulders they were protected from the wind. After the lantern was out and their eyes adjusted to the darkness, they could make out a few shapes below, like the roof of the schoolhouse. Sounds carried well up and down the valley. They heard his horse whinny and some cattle lowing up toward Fred's place. After exploring the rocks near them, Blackie settled in Minta's lap, purring contentedly, as if spending a night outdoors on top of a rocky hill were an everyday occurrence.

Every hoot of an owl, every coyote cry caused Minta to sit up in alarm. Expecting to hear sounds below, she strained her ears to try to distinguish whether what she was hearing were normal night noises or something else. She shifted her weight, trying to get comfortable on the hard ground. Her feet were going to sleep because of the cat on her lap and her crossed legs.

"Shh," Silas whispered, his hand tense on her shoulder. "I hear something." He'd been straining his ears as much as she had.

She listened: the faint creak of saddle leather, a hoof fall, a snort, as someone on horseback rode slowly and quietly into the schoolyard. She tried to see through the blackness, but shadows swam before her eyes and didn't coalesce into anything identifiable.

She jumped at a sound that could only be her cabin door being kicked open. A flicker of light—a match probably—showed at one window. Then more steady light appeared as candles were found and lit. He was in there, searching her cabin. She trembled at the thought of what would have happened had she been in bed asleep when he kicked in the door.

Silas reached around and circled her shoulders with his arm. "It's all right, Minta," he said softly. "You're safe up here. He'll go away soon when . . . ." He was interrupted by the sound of breaking glass as if something heavy had been thrown through her window.

Silas stood up to try to see better. A brighter glow was coming from the cabin. Too bright. "Oh no! The miserable bastard! He's set your cabin on fire!"

Minta's stomach heaved, and she was shaking uncontrollably. She had seen Edmund angry, and she had seen him mean. She'd never seen him so out of control that he would set fire to a house. If he had fallen that far, what might he have done to Lulabelle and Frank? She took some deep breaths to get herself under control, set Blackie on a rock, and managed to stand beside Silas. She could see the red glow from the cabin growing as she watched. "What can we do?" she asked.

"Nothing," Silas said. "Not a durn thing, pardon my French. It's going up fast. He must have found the lantern oil and spread it around. By the time we got there, and with so little water close by, it would be too late. All we can do is sit here and watch it burn. But we're witnesses. I'll go to the sheriff tomorrow and have him arrested for arson."

"If he can be found," she said, "and if the sheriff believes us. We can't really see who it is from this far away, although I *know* it's him. Surely he'll leave now. Someone might see the fire and come. Yes—see! I can see him silhouetted by the flames. He's leaving. No, he's . . . oh no!—not the school, too! Not my school!" The figure below was walking toward the schoolhouse, carrying a burning log from the cabin. Minta started to squeeze through the crevice. "I won't let him do this. We've got to do something to stop him, Silas."

"All right. Come on—it's two against one. Maybe we can stop him before the school goes up," he said as he passed her and started down the rocky slope. "We can't take the lantern, so be careful going down. You can feel your way until we're past the rocks, then just keep going downhill. As we get closer, the light from the cabin will help."

"Wait, Silas. I'll go first and distract him. Then you can come up behind him."

"No! That's too dangerous. I won't let you . . ."

"You're not *letting* me. I make my own decisions," she said, echoing his earlier sentiments. "Oh, we don't have time to argue. I wish you had a gun, or at least your rope."

"I took it off my horse and hung it on a fencepost before we took him down to the stream. I may have time to circle around and grab it, if he doesn't get to you too soon. This is the first time I wished I carried a gun since . . . well, I wish I had one. We'll make do. Now, save your breath until we get down there. Don't get to Edmund too soon. Give me time to get around behind him."

The first log Edmund carried to the school was slowly smoldering where he had thrown it on the roof. He was going back for another. He kicked open the woodshed door and emerged carrying a long piñon log covered with pitch on one end. He held that end of the log into the flames. When it was going good, he started back slowly toward the school. He held the log up toward one of the windows, preparing to throw it through. Minta was almost to the bottom of Rockytop where the hill flattened into the softball meadow.

"Edmund!" she yelled loudly across the ball field. "Edmund! I'm over here!"

He turned toward her, but she was still invisible in the darkness, as his eyes were adjusted to the flames he'd been looking at. He started toward the sound of her voice using the flaming log as a torch. Looking past him, she saw a figure dart across the schoolyard between the cabin and woodshed. Silas picked up his rope and began running toward them.

Minta knew he was good with a rope from horseback. She'd seen that when she'd watched him working cattle around the valley. But on foot, in the dark, and with a target so tall compared to a small cow, she wasn't sure he'd be able to be successful on the first try. She didn't want to think what would happen if he wasn't. The gap between Edmund and her was closing much more rapidly than the gap between Edmund and Silas.

Edmund wasn't running, just walking toward her with determination, holding the log in front of him. He climbed carefully over the back fence as she crossed the meadow toward him. Minta stopped. Silas had said not to get to Edmund too quickly. It was hard to stand there and wait as Edmund's form grew larger and more menacing as he approached. She could see him clearly, the burning cabin behind him lighting up the night sky, the burning log in his hand casting weird shadows across his face. He could see her, too, now.

"So, you decided to quit running, I see," Edmund said as he walked toward her. "Smart move. Maybe I'll go a little easy on you tonight." He laughed. "Maybe. I think we'd have time to do it on the teacher's desk before the school building goes up, don't you? Of course, you might not make it out of the burning building. Too bad—the teacher dying as she tried to save the school. But if you ask real nice, if you get down on your knees and beg me, maybe I'll let you come out with me. Maybe I'll let you come home with me. Not before your pretty little face gets scarred with the fire, though." He thrust the log's flaming end toward her. "If your face is so ugly you're ashamed to show it in public, that will keep you home with me forever, won't it?"

She jerked her head back involuntarily as the flame's warmth reached her, trying not to listen to his words. She kept her eyes focused on Edmund so she wouldn't betray the movement behind him—the rope circling in the air, the arm thrusting forward as the loop was thrown. She didn't know which of the three of them was more surprised when the rope slipped neatly around Edmund's chest and arms, sending the log crashing onto the ground as the loop pulled tight with a jerk from behind. He staggered and fell backwards, cursing as he hit the ground. Silas was on top of him immediately, completing the tying of his feet with the other end of the rope. Edmund lay like a hog-tied steer in a rodeo, flopping on the ground.

Minta stomped out a small fire the log had started in the dried weeds still left from last year. Fortunately, the new May grass coming up was moist and didn't catch fire.

"Water, Minta," Silas yelled. "Get buckets. The school roof's about to go!"

She ran toward the well and saw a figure running toward her. Paulo Valori, still in his nightclothes, ran to help her with the buckets. There was one at the well and two others she retrieved from just inside the cloakroom. Her own, of course, was gone with the cabin. Still, the three of them had the spot on the roof of the school put out by the time Fred's family arrived. The cabin and all its contents were a total loss. Paulo explained he'd gotten up to use the outhouse and saw the flames. He sent Sophie to alert Fred before running toward the school.

Silas helped Minta retrieve her belongings from Rockytop and put them in the schoolhouse. Blackie followed them back down and rubbed against Minta's legs until she picked him up. Paulo guarded Edmund while Fred went to get his wagon. The men lifted Edmund into the back of it. By then, the first rays of morning were beginning to lighten the sky, and Fred and Silas began the long drive to town to take Edmund to the sheriff.

Minta didn't know how long a jail sentence he would get for arson, or whether he would face charges in Indiana for assaulting Lulabelle and Frank. She could tell what he'd said to her, and maybe they would add some time for attempted murder. She would have a period of time free of him. But unless he was given life without parole, it wouldn't be long enough. She would always know he was coming after her, sometime. And he knew where she was now. She'd have to leave again. And this time, she wouldn't be able to tell anyone where she was or write her family or anyone here. She would have to disappear into this vast western wilderness and make whatever kind of life she could for herself. By herself.

But first she had to face whatever the community decided about her. It wouldn't be fair to them for her to run off before answering for her behavior. In the unlikely event they wanted her to finish out the school year, she would. Surely, she'd be safe from Edmund for that long, at least. And, if she were lucky, the people of the community would forgive her. Silas's forgiveness had felt so good, she longed for the same from the families of Rockytop.

She had refused to go home with Fred's family, saying she needed to stay in the school to make sure nothing rekindled. There was still a meeting scheduled there for the next night. It was past the time she normally got up for the day, but she unrolled the bedroll on the floor under the windows and tried to sleep. Even as tired as she was, she dozed only fitfully—a few minutes here, a few minutes there. By the time the sun reached its noon peak, she'd given up on sleep and prepared to meet whatever this day, and the next, would bring.

CHAPTER NINETEEN

More Revelations

⚜

Thursday, May 6, 1920—*Well, at least I still have the belongings I came with, plus a few more. Most of my food was stored in the dugout along with the large tub I use for bathing and laundry, both of which I feel I need badly after yesterday. I can cook on the stove in the school and sleep on the floor here. It's only for a few more weeks, if they even want me to stay that long. They may well decide tonight that I should go immediately. I will try to accept whatever they decide with dignity.*

I feel like I am waking from a long nightmare, but it isn't over yet; I know that. It won't be over until one of us is dead, or Edmund is locked up for life. All I can hope for is a respite during which I can gather my resources and attempt to find a place where I will be safe. Or, I may have to return to Indiana if the sheriff can't find out what happened to Lulabelle and Frank, or if he does find out and they need my help. I can't turn my back on them after all they've done for me. I have no doubt they have suffered at Edmund's hand. I'm not worried about Edmund's farm or animals—his brothers can take care of both. I won't ever go back to that cursed place, the home of my unhappiness.

I have a few hours until the meeting that will decide my immediate fate. I'll clean up myself and the school as well as possible. The smoke smell is still everywhere, and there's some water damage on several desks from what came through the hole burned in the roof. People had been commenting about how nice the school and grounds looked just the other day. Now all is a blackened mess. I have caused so much trouble for these people. I'm sure they will want me to leave.

Matthew Post arrived before the others and met Minta on the step. "This came for you after I'd left to come here the other day," he said, handing her a telegram. "I suspect if it had been a little earlier, we might have avoided some of this trouble." He gestured to the schoolyard and the remains of her cabin.

She read the telegram from Frank: *Minta, Edmund on his way there. Stop. Leave immediately. Stop. I am recovering. Stop. Lulabelle expected to live. Stop. Letter follows. Stop. Not your fault. Stop. Frank*

She handed the telegram to Matthew wordlessly. He read it. "I expect Mo—Sheriff Upton—will have more information for you. He's been telegraphing back and forth. He even went to Durango and used a telephone to call someone back in Indiana."

She finally found her voice. "I must go back there! Lulabelle expected to live? What does that mean? What did Edmund do to her? She must need my help! If she needs long-term care, then I . . ."

"Slow down, Minta. The telegram said a letter is coming. At least wait to see what the letter says. I'm sure that will give more information. Don't go running off before you find out what you'll be running to."

"Or if they even want to see me again, after what I've done to them," she said.

"He said it's not your fault. And it isn't."

"Of course it is. I brought this on them, and on all of the people here, too. If I hadn't . . ."

"Minta," Matthew said firmly, "do you think your parents are responsible for anything you have done? For lying to us and changing your name, for example?"

"My parents? Of course not! I mean, I was mad at them at first, because they encouraged me to marry Edmund. But I see now that they had no way of knowing what kind of man he was. And everything I've done here, I've done all on my own."

"Exactly. Your parents aren't responsible for your actions, and you are not responsible for Edmund's. He's a man with free choice to make good or bad decisions, on his own."

"But if I hadn't come here . . ."

"You had to be somewhere. I, for one, am thankful it was somewhere with people like Silas and Claudia to help you. Edmund is in jail, at least. Now, wipe your eyes and put on a pretty face. Here come the troops."

The crowd that filed into the school was grim-faced and tired-looking. Two meetings in three days was unprecedented, and the sight of the burned cabin and damaged school was sobering. Several people asked Minta if she needed anything—clothing, bedding, food. She said she didn't know yet. Angus came in with his mother. The other children had been left with Honor and Sophie at the Valoris' cabin.

They waited for Sheriff Upton to arrive. When he did, everyone let him speak first.

"I'm sure you all want to know the current status of the prisoner," he said, referring to Edmund. "He's in my jail awaiting the arrival of a deputy from Indiana to take him back there."

"What about trying him for arson here?" Paulo shouted. "I'd like to see him sent up for a long time."

"So would I," the sheriff answered. "But I'm afraid he might get a sympathetic judge here, and the charges in Indiana are worse."

"Sympathetic?" Claudia asked. "Who would be sympathetic about arson and attempted murder?"

"You heard how nice he can talk the other night," the sheriff answered. "All he'd have to do is convince the judge he was upset about his wife running away and accidentally knocked over a candle searching her cabin. And the murder threat would just be her word against his."

"And I suppose a woman's word isn't as good as a man's?" Claudia demanded.

"Now, Claudia—I didn't say that. But a judge might *think* it."

"What charges is he facing in Indiana?" Fred asked.

"Assault and battery. Breaking and entering. Attempted murder."

"What do you know about the condition of my relatives?" Minta asked. "What did he do to them?"

"From what I understand, he broke into their house when the woman was there alone and tied her to the bed. When she refused to tell him anything, in spite of his . . . treatment of her, he decided to wait for the man to come home, hid behind the bedroom door, and hit him over the head with a heavy object, then tied him up. When the man regained consciousness, he, Edmund, threatened to . . ." He paused, looking at the women in the audience. "To, um, 'mistreat' the woman if her husband didn't tell him where she was." He pointed to Minta, who was using all her self-control not to scream and cry, wanting to hear everything the sheriff said.

The sheriff continued, "Of course, the man told him." People in the audience nodded in agreement. A man would do whatever he had to in order to spare his wife. "The next day, when the man didn't show up for work, one of his friends came and found them. They'd both been knocked unconscious and left to die. They've been in the hospital, and it took awhile for the man to regain his memory of what happened. But the woman . . ." He paused again, looking uncertainly at Minta.

"What about Lulabelle? What is her condition?" she asked.

"She was in a coma for a time, severe head trauma. But she's awake now and doing a little better each day. She doesn't remember much, if any, of what happened."

"I must go back there and help her," Minta said.

"Wait for the letter that's coming," Matthew reminded her. "In the meantime, you," he gestured to the audience, "need to decide what's to be done about the rest of the school year. Do you want her to continue, if she's able, depending on her family situation? And what about next year? Shall I advertise for a new . . ."

"Of course, we want her to continue . . ." Rachel started.

"Not so fast," Fred interrupted. "We can't overlook the fact that she misrepresented herself and signed her contract with a false name. What kind of message would we be sending to the kids if . . ."

"What kind of message would we be sending if we throw her out now?" Hannah shouted.

Angry words were tossed back and forth, several people trying to talk at once. Matthew banged on the desk for order. "I'd like to say something," he said. "After Edmund Skraggs told me about Minta, I checked into the documentation she'd given me when she applied for the job. Her school didn't have a record of an Ella Jane Skraggs, but a kind professor offered that he remembered an Ella Jane Morgan. Was that your maiden name, Minta?"

"Yes."

"Then everything she said about herself, except her name, is true. She graduated with honor from a fine teaching college and had very good recommendations from her professors and the school where she did her practice teaching. She's more highly qualified than anyone else we've had here. I'm willing to overlook the name problem in light of the rest of it."

Several in the audience nodded agreement.

"I don't know," Fred said. "Lying to us about her circumstances . . . "

Angus walked to the front of the room and tapped his uncle on the shoulder. "Can—I mean, may—I say something?" he asked. "I mean, the kids—the other kids—they said since I was at the other meeting, I should come to this one. We have something to say."

"Let the kid talk," Ernst said.

Fred stepped away and left Angus in the center of the room. Angus raised his head and looked directly at Minta, as she'd told him to do at the Christmas program, so he wouldn't see all the other eyes on him.

"You all keep saying she's a liar," Angus started, "but she's not. She used a different name, but a lot of you do, too. Like, I know Mr. Archuleta's real name isn't Archie, but you all call him that. And Mr. Rickerts won't allow anyone to call him his real first name, whatever it is. I heard people talking about that. What's more important is that she doesn't lie about anything else. Whatever she says she'll do, she does. We always know what to expect because she's fair and honest. And she teaches us good," he stopped. "Or is it well?" Minta nodded at him, smiling.

"Well. She teaches us well," Angus restated.

"Angus," Rachel said. "A year ago, could you have gotten up and said a speech like that in front of everyone?"

"No! I would've died first. She taught me I could."

"Exactly," Rachel said. "Fred, I never stand up to you, but I am now. You're wrong. Listen to the children. *Your* children. *Our* children."

"I have no quarrel with her as a teacher," Fred said. "But I'm still concerned that she came here under false pretenses . . ."

"Oh for heaven's sake, Fred," Claudia said. "The West is full of people who came here under false pretenses."

"The whole country is," Paulo said. "My mother would never tell me what my grandfather did in Italy, but he brought his family here one step ahead of the law. He wasn't proud of his past, but he made a good new life for us in this country."

"Truth be told," Jens said, "a lot of us may have come here to get away from things in our past."

Hannah stood and put her hand on Jens' arm. "You don't have to tell, Jens," she said.

"No, I want to," he said. "I . . . we . . . had a good life back in Enid. I had the biggest grocery in town, and we had a nice new two-story house on the best street. Then the town fell on hard times. A lot of my customers couldn't pay. I extended credit to too many people who never came through. Then I couldn't pay my creditors. Finally we lost it all— the store, the house. I heard there was some land opened up for home-steading out here, so we decided to make a fresh start. Our older girls, they had married back there, so they stayed. But Ernst and his wife came with us—the Fredrickson name was no good there any more." He stopped abruptly and sat down.

In the awkward silence that followed, Mr. Rickerts said, "Algernon, Angus. If your given name was Algernon, would you let people call you that? When I was a boy, other kids called me 'Algie.' Now, I know you all call me 'Old Man' Rickerts. Beats Algernon."

A few people laughed as Silas walked to the front of the room. "And my name isn't Silas Tower," he said, turning to face them. "It's Clay . . . Clayton Calhoun." He looked sideways at the sheriff.

"Is that supposed to mean something to me?" Mo Upton asked.

"I don't know. I thought it might," Silas said. "Every time I go someplace with a post office, I look for my picture, but so far . . ."

"You might want to stop right there, boy," Mo said, "before you say something I might have to do something about."

"No. I want to say it. I want to stop running. It's kind of a long story," he paused, but no one else suggested he not continue; all eyes were riveted on him. "My stepfather was a mean man, a lot like that Edmund Skraggs. When he started in on hitting me with his fists instead of his belt, I ran away from home. Ended up in Laramie, cowboying for an outfit south of town. Well, every Friday we got our pay and hit the saloon. Another outfit had some boys that didn't like our outfit. We got into an argument with them in the saloon, and the barkeep threw us out and told us to finish it in the street.

"Well, we was pushing and swinging our fists as much as we could, considering how drunk we all was, when one guy from that other outfit pulled out a gun and pointed it at one of our guys. I was the closest to him, so I grabbed his arm, tried to take away the gun. I don't really know what happened—who pulled the trigger—but it went off. Next thing I know he's lying there in the street, and my buddies are telling me to run.

"Spent the night in a barn and woke up the next morning with a hangover and no clear recollection of what happened. My friend came and said the guy was dead, and the sheriff was looking for me. I was all of seventeen then. A dumb kid. I got on my horse and started riding south. Somewhere north of Denver, I ran into a farmer in a field. He asked if I wanted to work for my room and board. I was hungry, so I said okay. He asked my name. I'd already decided on Silas—my mother always talked about her favorite uncle Silas. So I said, 'Silas,' and he said, 'Silas what?' I'd been following the railroad tracks, and we was standing in the shade of a water tower. So I said, 'Tower.' That's how I come to be Silas Tower. Minta ain't—isn't—the only one can change her name.

"Anyway, I stayed there and each place afterwards just long enough to get enough money and strength to go on. I quit drinking, too. Haven't had a drop since then. And I never carry a gun unless I'm going out hunting. Anyway, I kept going south. Finally ended up near Santa Fe. Was cowboying for an outfit there when Rickerts found me."

He turned and looked at Mr. Rickerts. "I won't blame you now if you want to go back on giving me your place. It probably ain't legal anyway, since I didn't sign my real name."

Mr. Rickerts snorted. "Heck no, I don't want to go back on the deal. I give it to who you is now. I don't care what you done when you was a dumb kid. Haven't you been listening to these people? The great thing about this country is we give people a second chance. We'll go back to the lawyer and sign papers again with your real name, make sure it's all legal."

"Hold on, now," Mo said. "Nobody better be signing anything. I'm going to have to do something about this."

"I know, Sheriff; I want you to," Silas said. "Like I said, I'm tired of looking over my shoulder all the time and expecting to see my ugly mug in the post office. You can arrest me now, if you want, but I wouldn't advise putting me in the same cell with Edmund Skraggs. I wouldn't be responsible for what I might do to . . ."

"Let me make some inquiries with the law in Laramie first," Mo said. "Case may be closed by now. I'll trust you not to run off until I've found out if you need to go up there and straighten things out. Sounds like whatever you did was involuntary, so the main trouble you'd be in is for running from the law."

Silas sat down next to Rickerts and hung his head. The old man put his hand on Silas's shoulder.

"Well, this has certainly been a night of revelations," Claudia said. "Just when you think you know your neighbors . . ."

"Yes," Fred said. "Now we'd better get down to the business we came here for. I'm willing to go with a majority vote of the people here and skip having to have another board meeting right away, if that meets with everyone's approval."

So it was decided that Minta would finish out the school year. She refused to commit to more than that until she heard from Frank and Lulabelle. She also refused several offers to go live with various families, preferring to stay in the school with Blackie and her few remaining belongings.

The next morning, Fred showed up with a folding cot so she didn't have to sleep on the floor. "I'm glad the vote went the way it did, Minta," he said.

"Are you?"

"Yes. I know we haven't always gotten along, but I like—respect—what you've done here with the students. And, yes, I know about the ball and Robert. You can't keep stuff like that quiet here. I played the devil's advocate last night so that if there was anyone who had objections they'd feel free to make themselves known. Sometimes people are afraid to speak up."

"People sure spoke up last night," she said.

He laughed. "Yes, they did. I hope everything turns out all right for Silas. He's a good man. And for you."

CHAPTER TWENTY

Gracious in Victory

Sunday, May 9, 1920—I have finally convinced Silas that he has no hope with me. I'm afraid he left angry last night. He seemed to think that, since Edmund is going to jail, I am free. I pointed out to him that I'm still married, and my husband is still alive. Silas said he could take me to stay with his aunt in Nevada, that if I live and work there for six weeks to establish residency, I can go to a judge and ask for a divorce. If Edmund doesn't show up and object, which he won't since he'll be incarcerated, it will be granted. I told him I had no intention of being a divorced woman. I've already broken enough commandments. All I can do now is hope to be forgiven and try to live the rest of my life blamelessly. I also told him that I would not wish to marry a man who wanted to marry a divorced woman. That's when we had words and he left in anger. So now I have what I wanted all along: a life free of men. Edmund is on his way to jail, Luke is moving away, and Silas is no longer a part of my life.

Getting back into the routine of school was difficult, but I feel we have now managed. The students wanted to know what they should call me now. I said that, as far as they were concerned, I was still Miss Mayfield and that they still have to prepare for the end-of-school tests and the softball tournament. That got their minds off my situation, and they went back to ball practice with a vengeance. I've been talking to them a lot about how to be gracious in victory and in defeat. I hope they have taken my words to heart because, either way, their character will be tested.

Minta put down her pen, blew on the page until she was sure the ink was dry, and closed her diary. She heard hoofbeats outside. It was hard not to always expect either Silas or Edmund whenever she heard a horse, and her heart raced as she went to the window. But it was neither—it was the sheriff. What now? Had theft charges been filed against her after all?

"Good day, ma'am," he said as he dismounted.

"Come in, Sheriff."

"Call me 'Mo.' Short for Moses. 'Most everyone else does." He stood awkwardly holding his hat in one hand. She could add him to the ranks of grown men who seemed to feel awkward in the schoolroom. She took his hat and offered him her desk chair.

"All right, Mo," she said. "And you call me 'Minta.' Do you have business with me today?" She sat on the recitation bench.

"I'm afraid so." He looked down at his hands. I have some . . . news. I'm not sure . . . "

"Lulabelle! Is she all right? She hasn't taken a turn . . ."

"No. It's not her. It's Edmund."

"What about him? He should be back in Indiana by now."

"Well, they were on the way. I told that deputy that he was a sneaky bas . . . cuss . . . and to watch out for him, but . . . "

"He's escaped, hasn't he? I knew I'd never be safe from him." She jumped up and turned in a full circle, looking around the room, taking inventory. "Please leave, Mo. I must pack immediately. He'll be on his way back here to . . ."

"No, no. Let me tell you the rest. The deputy kept him handcuffed like I said, but when he went to the lavatory on the train, he didn't want Edmund in that small space with him. He cuffed him to the railing on the deck between cars just outside the lavatory. Well, apparently he didn't notice the railing had a crack in it, and Edmund managed to jerk the metal apart and slip the cuffs off of the rail."

"Could you hurry up and tell me the rest? I told you. I need to pack and get out of here." She was already mentally planning what to take and what to leave.

"No, you don't. I'm trying to tell you—Edmund jumped off the train there, somewheres in Missouri. It was a pretty steep bank, and he couldn't break his fall with his hands still cuffed. He rolled to the bottom and hit the rocks. There was a lot of blood."

"But where is he now? How is he?"

"We don't know. We assume he's dead because . . ."

"You what? You don't *know!*" She tried to keep the hysteria out of her voice, but her shaking hands betrayed her.

"Calm down, Minta." Mo stood and put his hands on her shoulders. "Let me finish telling you. The engineer refused to stop the train right there, because they were almost to the next station. The deputy got off there and rounded up a posse. They rode back to look for Edmund, or his body. Like I said, there was a lot of blood. He must've took a beating bouncing down that bank. They followed the blood trail to the stream at the bottom of the canyon there."

"But they didn't find him," she said with resignation in her voice, turning away from him and wrapping her arms around herself.

"The locals call that stream 'Devil's Creek.' It looks like you can get across it, but if you try, it grabs you and sucks you under. It seldom gives up its victims, either. There's so many submerged logs and large rocks for a body to get trapped under. Unless there's a drought and the water level goes way down, they never find the bodies. That's probably what happened to Edmund. They followed his trail to the river, and then it just disappeared. That posse rode up and down both sides of the stream and never saw any more signs. No more blood. No footprints. They're getting wanted posters printed up now. They're going to put them up back there in Missouri and in Indiana and out here, too, in case he does come back—but, like I said, we all think he's dead."

"Okay. As *I* said, Mo, I need to pack. If he didn't die, he'll be on his way back here."

"Where will you go?"

"I haven't decided yet. And when I do, I won't tell anyone here. You've seen what Edmund will do to find out what he wants to know."

Mo scratched his chin. "Yep. And what's to stop him from doing it to people who don't know nothing? He don't know who knows and who don't. If you think your leaving will protect people here . . ."

Minta looked stricken. "I never thought of that. Of course, he'd try to get information from anyone who knew me. All the people here . . . my, my children . . . ." Minta sat down heavily at her desk. She couldn't hold back the tears any more. If she stayed, she'd be in danger. If she left, all her friends and neighbors would be. Maybe she should just give herself up to Edmund.

Mo walked to the windows and looked out at the peaceful valley, giving her time to compose herself. Finally he turned back to her. "Don't go running off right away, Minta. Take some time to think on it. Even if he did survive and escape detection somehow, he's badly injured. He'd have to have some broken bones, and probably a head injury, too. He won't be back here any time soon, if at all." He turned to the stove. "I see you got a pan of what smells like coffee heated. Mind if I have a cup?"

Minta stood up. "Of course not. Where are my manners? This is my only pan left after the fire. I've been using it to make coffee. I have to have my coffee," she forced a laugh. "Here." She took one of the cups from the water pail and poured coffee from the sauce pan into it. "Careful, that tin handle gets hot. I use a rag to hold it."

Mo took off his bandana and wrapped it around the cup and sipped slowly. Minta poured herself a cup, too, and was glad to see her hands had stopped shaking. The only sound for several minutes was Mo blowing and sipping loudly. He set his cup down. "You know, Minta, people here will help you. If you let them."

She looked into his kind eyes. "I know, Mo. I'm just not sure there's anything anyone can do. I will take your advice and think about it before I leave. You're right. I should be safe for several weeks anyway. And I do want to finish the school term and go to the last-day picnic. I owe the students that much."

"It's not about what you owe, Minta. It's about you being able to live your life. It's about running. Sometime, someplace you've got to quit running. Like Silas. Why not here? Let Edmund come back, if he's alive; let him get arrested. They'll put him away for a long, long time, now."

He drained his cup and stood up. "Speaking of running, I'd better hit the road. I've got some news for Silas, too. Good news."

"Oh?" Minta tried not to act too interested.

"Guess he wouldn't mind my telling, since it's good. I heard from Laramie, and that case was closed a long time ago. After talking to the witnesses, they declared it an accidental shooting. They don't want Silas to go back up there."

"I'm sure he'll be pleased to hear that he's in the clear," Minta said. If the sheriff so readily shared Silas's news with her, he would probably tell Silas and other people about her new troubles. Well, it couldn't be helped. Soon everyone would know. She'd have to decide what to do, and soon.

As the sheriff left, he handed her a letter from Frank. She tore it open as he mounted his horse and was engrossed in reading when he rode away.

Dear Minta,

First, we are hopeful Lulabelle will recover fairly well. She may not get all her memory back and we're having to reteach her quite a bit, but she's learning fast. The doctor says that's fairly common with severe head injuries. I guess I'm a lot more hardheaded than she is. I haven't had any problems, except headaches. Your parents are here, and they have been a big help to me with her and with everything else. We all agree you must not blame yourself. You did what you had to do in a bad situation. No one could have known, even you, how violently Edmund would react. I spoke to his older brother, who said Edmund always had a bad temper and was often in trouble as a child for playing with fire and deliberately hurting animals. They thought getting married would be good for him, settle him down. How wrong they were. The brother said to tell you they are sorry you were the brunt of the failed experiment.

I don't know whether this will find you still there, or if you got the telegram and are fleeing from Edmund. I hope the information I have given will lead to his arrest fairly quickly, so you don't have to keep running. If you ever feel you can, we would welcome you back here. But don't feel you have to come, and don't come right away. We are managing fine, and the doctor says the less extra stimulation Lulabelle has for a while, the better. She needs her established routine with your mother and me until she's more ready to face the rest of the world.

My best wishes for your safety and good health. Frank

Of course, Frank had written the letter before he knew of Edmund's capture, much less his escape. It was frustrating not to be able to go to Lulabelle. Minta could help with reteaching her. That much, at least, she could do for her cousin. But now, with Edmund possibly still out there somewhere, she couldn't go back to Frank and Lulabelle's, either. She couldn't put them in more danger after what they'd already suffered.

Minta pulled her Bible across the desk toward her. She'd promised Mo she would think about what to do. Her grandmother had taught her to do her thinking with a Bible in hand. She opened to Second Corinthians. She always liked to read the advice Paul gave to new Christians. It helped her to know people had been struggling with the same issues since Christianity began. In spite of the turmoil of the last few minutes, she felt strangely calm. When she got to the fourth chapter, she paused and reread the eighth and ninth verses:

We are troubled on every side, yet not distressed; we are perplexed, but not in despair; Persecuted, pursued yet not forsaken; cast down, but not destroyed . . .

That described her. She was troubled and pursued. Yet she felt calm. There was hope. That reminded her of something she'd read recently in Romans, and she turned back in her Bible, finding the passage in he fifth chapter:

> *. . . let us rejoice in tribulations also: knowing that tribulation worketh patience; And patience, experience; and experience, hope: And hope maketh us not ashamed; because the love of God is shed abroad in our hearts . . . . But where sin abounded, grace did much more abound: That as sin hath reigned unto death, even so might grace reign through righteousness unto eternal life by Jesus Christ our Lord.*

Really, whatever happened, it was all right, since she would have eternal life. And now, on this earth, she could have grace. Her grandmother had tried to explain grace to her. She felt as if only now she was starting to understand it.

"Put your problems in perspective," her grandmother also said. When she looked at the big picture, her time with Edmund was just a small, dirty smudge on the white cloth of her faith. And her faith would be sufficient for whatever came her way. She wouldn't abandon her friends, at least not yet.

She closed the Bible. She still had much to do. First, she put a chair under the door knob so no one could come in and surprise her. She could escape out a window, if need be. She would trust in the Lord, but she'd also do what she could to protect herself. In fact, the next time she went to town, she'd buy a gun and ask someone to teach her how to use it. Second, she would write Frank and warn him about Edmund's escape. Surely Edmund wouldn't return to the scene of his crime where he was wanted for attempted murder, but Frank needed to be told. Third, she had to finish her lesson plans for the last weeks of school.

After all, she was still Minta Mayfield, teacher. Even though everyone now knew she was really Ella Jane Skraggs, she had decided to remain Minta. She liked Minta so much better—the person as well as the name. Ella had been a young, naive girl who thought the world should arrange itself to suit her. Minta was a woman, still growing and maturing, of course, but becoming more confident in her abilities to take care of herself and others, with God's help.

CHAPTER TWENTY-ONE

Gracious in Defeat

ﾠﾠﾠﾠﾠﾠ

Sunday, May 30, 1920—*All is ready for my last day of school. It's even more bittersweet than I expected, because I don't know when—or even if—I will be returning here. Matthew has graciously allowed me until July 1st to let him know if I wish to return next year. Everyone is encouraging me to stay, in spite of the situation with Edmund. With each day that passes without word from or about him, I grow more hopeful that he did perish in Devil's Creek—a fitting end for a man so controlled by the Dark One.*

All week we have been taking end-of-the-year tests. Overall, I'm pleased with my students' progress this year, although I can see areas and individuals that still need improvement. I wonder if other teachers ever feel competent, or if the end of every year leaves them feeling they haven't done enough. I wonder what kind of teacher I would have been if I could have concentrated fully on teaching, without all this business with Edmund.

Silas continues to keep his distance. I can't say I blame him. We said harsh words to each other the last time we spoke alone. Last night I thought I saw him sitting on his horse on the hill overlooking the valley. At first it gave me a start, because he was holding a gun, and I was afraid it was Edmund. Silas never carries a gun. But the figure just sat quietly watching over the valley until I drifted off to sleep. I wonder . . . I need to stop wondering. Grandmother always said, "The saddest words are 'it might have been'."

Minta kept the last day of school moving along quickly. She didn't want to dwell on "lasts." She had assigned the students a final day speech. They were each to stand up and tell the best thing they had learned in school this year. She told them she would grade them on their presentation as well as the content of their speeches. Angus's experiences had convinced her that they all needed to learn to get up and speak in front of others early and often.

The first and second graders mostly talked about learning to read. LaQuita happily said she could now read to Wanda and Jaime. Wendell said that, at first, he didn't want to learn to read because he was afraid Florence and their father would stop reading to him then, and he really, really liked to be read to. But he found out even big kids got read to in school, so it was all right if he still got read to at home, too. Dale, however, said the main thing he learned was new ideas for building play "fahms" in the corner of the schoolyard. At least he was honest.

Gertie said she learned that girls were at least as smart as boys. She stopped just short of saying smarter. And that they could play softball just as well, if they wanted to practice. Gunner had found a new enthusiasm for science and expounded at length on all he'd learned about the solar system.

Florence said tearfully that if she had to move to a new school she could still do well, because she learned to work on her own and to help younger kids with their work. Robert smiled his sly grin that Minta had learned to look out for and said, "Well, I learned what a ferule is used for." When the laughter died down, he said he also learned a lot of math and that he wasn't afraid of math any more.

Angus said, "You know what I've learned. I'm doing it now. I learned if you have something to say, you should get up and say it, even if it's hard to do. I learned that bad things happen to people, even to adults, but they still have to go on living their lives—working, teaching, going to school—whatever. I learned that school isn't just a place you learn math and grammar. You can learn how to be a grownup here, too."

Minta wasn't sure she could trust her voice after that, but Honor saved her having to say anything by asking, "May I say what I learned, too? I know I'm not really a student, but . . ."

"Of course, Honor, go ahead." Minta smiled at her. Honor had come to school to enjoy the last day with them even though it wasn't a Wednesday.

"I learned," Honor said, "the two most important things I wanted forever to learn. I learned to read music and play the piano, and I learned what I want to do with the rest of my life. I want to be a teacher."

"Thank you, Honor," Minta said quickly before the girl launched herself into one of her lengthy monologues. "I'm sure you'll succeed."

"I think Honor should be able to play in the softball tournament tomorrow," Robert said. "She was kind of a student here this year. You taught her piano. And she's good. At softball, I mean. At least as good as Michael."

"No, Robert," Minta said. "We're not going to put any ringers on our team."

"What's a 'ringer'?" Robert asked.

"Somebody that's not supposed to be there," Angus answered.

"But since you brought up the game, tell me what you're going to do if you lose," Minta said.

The older boys sighed audibly while the younger pupils dutifully recited: "Shake hands with the other team and say, 'Congratulations, good game.'"

"And smile while you're doing it," Minta added. "And what are you going to do if you win?"

"The same thing," they answered.

"No, we won't," Michael said.

"Excuse me?" Minta asked. "Why not?"

"Because if we win, those guys from Halpern won't wait around to shake hands. They'll all run crying to their mommies."

Minta couldn't help joining in the laughter. When she got her face under control, she said, "Seriously. I expect you to be . . . "

"Gracious in victory, gracious in defeat!" they all shouted.

"Okay, okay. I guess that's one lesson you've learned. Now, when I was in town the other day, Mr. Post said we should have a nickname—a mascot—for our school. Like the lions or tigers, or something. All the schools are going to have one for the tournament this year."

After much discussion the students decided they wanted something that was native to the area where they lived. They discussed coyotes, mountain lions, black bears, deer, elk, and porcupines. Each choice had some problem with it—either they didn't think it was a tough enough image for the school, or they were afraid one of the other schools would pick it.

"I can just see all four schools picking coyotes," Michael said. "We've got to be different."

"What's different about Rockytop?" Mary asked.

"Just the snakes," Angus replied. "That's it! The Rockytop Rattlesnakes—no, the Rockytop Rattlers."

Everyone liked that name, especially Michael, who, as the best artist, was commissioned to draw and paint their banner. Snakes were easy to draw.

The day of the picnic couldn't have been a more perfect Rocky Mountain spring day. The sky was blue, the grass in the field next to the Halpern Methodist Church was green, and the breeze was warm and gentle.

Lots were drawn among the four schools to see who would play each other first. Game One was Shady Rest versus Halpern. Game Two would be Piñon Hollow versus Rockytop. Then everyone would eat their box lunches, take a half-hour rest, and assemble for the championship game between the winners of the first two games.

Each school had brought its own equipment, but the man from Liberty who was serving as umpire picked Rockytop's to use for the games. Theirs was the newest and best looking ball and bat. The Rockytop students thought that was a good omen for them, especially since Minta had had the idea to have Michael paint their rattlesnake symbol on the ball as well.

Michael and Angus had come to the picnic with their pockets full of rattlesnake rattles which they had been collecting whenever a snake was killed. They had enough for each child and Minta to have one, and, at a prearranged signal, they all rattled them together. It was their battle cry and, they hoped, would intimidate their opponents. There never was a team better prepared for a game, Minta thought, as she unfurled their pillowcase banner over the section of wooden benches assigned to them.

Minta sat with her kids to watch the Shady Rest Bobcats and the Halpern Coyotes play their game. It was no contest. Halpern had them outnumbered and outsized. The Shady Rest teacher hadn't found out until late in the term about the tournament and didn't really know how to help her students prepare for it. It was over quickly and time for Minta's group to take the field. They rattled their way out, creating a hair-raising sound to anyone who had spent any time in rattlesnake country.

At first, it looked like the Piñon Hollow Eagles and the Rockytop Rattlers were pretty evenly matched, even though one Piñon Hollow lad pointed out gleefully that eagles preyed on rattlesnakes. Piñon had more big kids, but they were mostly girls. It soon became apparent that they weren't at all interested in softball, and neither was their teacher, Claire Carpenter, who wasn't even watching the game. One girl dropped the ball when she broke a fingernail catching it, ignoring the shouts of her teammates to throw the ball home.

After a shaky start, Rockytop found its game and rolled to a decided victory. The Rockytop players were gracious until it came time to shake hands—it became obvious that some of the Piñon Hollow girls were more interested in flirting with Angus and Michael than in discussing the game. Then Minta's kids couldn't get away fast enough. They all sat together at lunch and plotted strategy based on what they'd seen during Halpern's game.

Minta was vaguely aware of community members around her as she watched the big match, but she was so intent on the game that she couldn't have said who they were. Each time one of her students went up to bat, she held her breath. The same thing happened when a ball was in the air wanting to be caught. She even forgot to keep rattling her rattle as she was supposed to do every time an opponent went to bat.

By the last inning, the score was tied at five each. Rockytop was at bat, and Gina was next up.

"Remember what to do," Angus told her as she lugged the heavy bat up to the plate.

"I'm afraid the ball will hit me again," she said, backing away from the plate.

"We talked about this already," Angus said. "You can do it. You're tough. Do it for the school, and for Miss Mayfield."

"Okay," Gina said reluctantly. She stepped up to the plate, hefted the bat to her shoulder, planted it there, crouched down, and waited. And waited.

"What's the holdup?" someone in the crowd yelled to the Halpern pitcher.

"I'm afraid I'll hit her again. She's too little," he yelled back. In the previous inning one of his pitches had grazed her arm and sent her walking to first base, crying, as the crowd booed their disapproval of his pitching.

"Just throw the ball," his catcher yelled. "I'll catch it."

The pitcher threw a slow, underhand pitch that went wide. Ball One. The next one was way high. Ball Two. The third didn't even make it to the plate, bouncing in front of it. Ball Three. Another wide outside ball, and Gina walked.

Robert was up next and sent a fly ball to left field. Gina made it to second, and he made it to first.

Then Dale was up. He swung at the first three pitches, missed them all, and was out.

Florence was next. They'd taught her to bunt, and she did, making it to first while Robert got to second. But Gina was tagged out at third.

Michael, next up, was their cleanup hitter. He hit a long fly past center field, a home run. Rockytop was ahead by three. It was a good thing because LaQuita was next and struck out. Now it all rested on what Halpern could or couldn't do in the last half of the last inning. And whether Rockytop could put three of them out before they did it.

Michael tried. He struck out the first batter. Then he caught a short fly ball from the second. Two away and no one on base. The interest level of the crowd was way up. It looked like Rockytop was going to pull an upset. Then the tide turned. The next three batters got on, and the bases were loaded. Minta vaguely heard the groans as the next batter stepped to the plate: Halpern's best hitter.

Angus stepped forward to talk to Michael. She knew they were discussing whether to walk the guy. They'd give up a run, but he wouldn't be able to hit all his runners in. In the end, they must have decided not to. Michael sent him honest pitches. He missed two and connected with a sickening smack on the third.

Robert, in center field, ran as if his life depended on it, but he couldn't get under the ball. It landed several yards beyond him and bounced into the bushes. Minta watched as the four Halpern runners rounded the bases and crossed home plate grinning and waving their hats, ending the longest, closest game anyone there had witnessed in recent memory.

She stood to applaud both teams, as did the rest of the crowd. After a brief, stunned hesitation, Angus, followed by Michael and then the rest of the team, walked over to the Halpern players and extended their hands mumbling "good game" and "congratulations." Minta smiled. They'd get them next year. Then—what was she thinking? She might not even be here next year. She became aware someone was speaking her name and turned to see Halpern's teacher, Ben Griffith.

"Wow, Minta," he said. "Your kids can play. I thought for a minute there you had us. Good job."

"Thank you, Ben," she said. Over his shoulder she saw Silas walking away with the rest of the crowd. He hadn't spoken to her the whole day.

She went looking for her students and gave each a quick hug, complimenting them on the game and their handling of the loss. "You did your best," she told them, "and that's what counts. I'm very proud of all of you."

"We'll beat them next year," Michael said. "You just watch."

She hadn't told them she might be leaving, and she didn't do so now. They were excited about starting their summer without school. They'd forget about her soon enough.

Matthew Post was waving at her, working his way through the few remaining celebrants. He held out a letter. "You know, Minta, if you come back next year, you really need to get your own post office box."

"Yes, I know. I'm sorry you've had to deal with my mail all year."

"I'm not complaining. Once they get a road automobiles can handle into Rockytop, you'll get Rural Free Delivery out here like the farmers down the valley do." He sounded like he expected her to be back. Well, it would partly depend on this letter. She sat down in the grass to read it.

Dear Minta,

Lulabelle still can't write very well, so asked me to pen this. You asked if you should come here. The answer is no. Lulabelle doesn't want to remain in this house any longer than necessary now that she has return-ing memories of what happened to us here—and now that we don't know the fate or whereabouts of Edmund, although I'm sure if he were alive we'd have found out by now. From the sale of our property here, we will be able to move and start over somewhere where I can make a go of my own dry goods store. Abottsville certainly doesn't need another one, and I wouldn't want to be in competition with my former employer anyway. I've been making inquiries. I corresponded with a man named Matthew Post. He says there's a nice little town in the Colorado mountains named Liberty that is growing rapidly and is in need of a dry goods establish-ment. He even knows of a vacant building that will be suitable with space on ground level for a store and a small apartment above for us. There's strength in numbers, Minta. I think we should all stick together.

So, Minta, don't come to us. We will come to you. I have convinced your parents to come with us, just for a visit. Maybe, eventually, they'll

be persuaded to move, too. We have much to do here first—selling every-
thing, buying stock for the store, and so forth. I will send a telegram when
I know the date we'll be making the move. Lulabelle will have a corner of
the store for a millinery shop. She has discovered a talent for making ladies'
hats, and the doctor says it's good therapy for her. Seeing you again will
also be good for her.

I rode down to your place and visited with Edmund's brothers. They
are keeping up the place and taking care of the animals. They were appalled
and ashamed when the wanted posters went up. I'm sure the gossips in the
town are working overtime. You said the family was reclusive. They're even
more so now. They did ask after you.

We remain faithfully yours, Frank and Lulabelle

Back at Rockytop, Minta put away all the books and supplies for
the last time and gave the blackboards a good double washing. Her bags
were mostly all packed. Tomorrow Fred was coming to take her to
Liberty. Posts had invited her to stay with them until she decided on
her course of action, and she'd been offered a temporary job at the grocery store while the owner's wife stayed home with a new baby.

At the picnic, Fred had told her the board decided not to rebuild
the teacherage. The teacher would have to stay with various families or
have another place to live. Minta had gotten used to her freedom and
independence. She wasn't sure she wanted to continue to teach here if
she had to board with families. Well, she'd discuss it with Matthew.
Maybe a job would open up at the Liberty School in the fall. She knew
of a couple teachers who ought to leave there for the good of the students. And then she'd be closer to Lulabelle, although she would miss
her own students and Rockytop terribly.

While she'd been living with Edmund as his wife, she had thought
nothing could be worse. Then when she ran away and was living a lie,
deceiving people she'd grown to love, facing life as the wife of a con-
victed felon, she thought that was worse. Now she knew what "worse"
was. It was not knowing where Edmund was or even if he were alive. It

was living her life in fear, always looking over her shoulder, starting at the slightest sound, keeping a chair under the doorknob whenever she was alone. One thing she'd learned, however, is you can't run away from your life. It follows you.

She was just getting ready to undress for bed when she looked out the window and saw the figure on horseback again. It must be Silas. What was he doing? She put her boots back on and started walking up the hill toward him. She thought he'd ride to meet her, but he didn't—just sat staring out at the valley, the road, the cattle.

He waited until she was all the way up to him before dismounting. "Hello, Minta. Are you still 'Minta'?"

"Yes, I wish to remain Minta. Forever. How about you? Are you still 'Silas'?"

"Yes, I guess so. It's easier, here. I did take the Calhoun name back, though, when I signed the property papers. I'm Clayton Silas Calhoun now."

"What are you doing out here every night? And why do you have a gun? You said you'd never carry a gun again."

"Things change. Mo said you didn't feel safe. I'm just trying to raise the safety level of this valley."

"Silas! You can't spend every night watching over me!"

"Excuse me, but when you refused to do what it takes to become free to marry me, you lost your right to tell me what I can and can't do. And besides, I don't do it alone. Richard Haley takes some shifts, and soon I think others will, too. Two nights ago, I stopped a mountain lion from taking a calf. It's more than just you we're protecting. It's our way of life."

Minta had tears in her eyes and didn't feel up to talking. Finally, Silas continued. "You know, after seven years—I think it's seven, anyway . . . I'll have to ask a lawyer—you can declare Edmund dead, even if they never find his body. Then you'd be free to start over, and we . . ."

"Stop, Silas. You sound like my students, always wanting do-overs. You can't always make everything work out the way you want it to. Just because the world has laws about divorce and missing people, that doesn't release me from my marriage vows. And you're young and have a ranch to take care of. Seven years is too long to wait. You should marry, have children . . ."

"Not unless you're their mother."

"That's not going to happen, Silas."

"Yes, I know how stubborn you are. Well, so am I. I'll be here, every night. If you ever want me, you know where to find me." He remounted and turned his horse to face up valley, checking the road in that direction.

She looked up at his stubborn back. She couldn't think of anything else to say, so she turned and began the long walk back to her schoolhouse. When she got inside, she didn't put the chair under the doorknob.

She thought again of staying here. She'd like to. Why was it so hard to know whether to follow her heart or her head? She'd thought she was following her head when she married Edmund. Her heart said she didn't love him; her head said he was a good catch and she would be a fool to turn down a successful older man. Well, see what that had gotten her? Maybe it was time to give her heart a try. She looked out the window and could still make out Silas's form in the spot where she'd left him. So close, yet so far away.

Afterword

꿏

June 1, 1920. Devil's Creek, Missouri.

Sari bent over, placing one hand on her aching back, and picked a handful of the wild mint that grew all around her cabin. Eddie seemed to have a fondness for mint; he was always mumbling about it in his delirium, so she fixed him mint tea and mint poultices for his wounds. Finally, it looked like he was going to live. At first she wouldn't have given him a snowball's chance at a Fourth of July picnic, but lately his periods of consciousness were longer, and the worst of the wounds were starting to heal. The swelling that had kept his eyes shut had gone down, and the broken nose stopped bleeding. She set the broken ankle herself. It was healing pretty good, considering, but he'd probably always have a limp.

He also had strange red wounds all around his wrists, as if he'd been hitting himself with rocks. She supposed he'd gotten those in the river, too. It could batter a person pretty good. It was a miracle he made it out of the water. Few who fell in did.

He still didn't seem to remember much about who he was or what happened to him. He didn't talk much when he was conscious. But, by piecing together what he said in his delirious state, she'd figured out his name was Edward Mayfield and he had come from Oregon. Something about a missionary. Maybe he was a missionary, or he'd been raised there by missionaries.

After her boy, Orville, found him down by the creek, they'd dragged him back to the house and taken care of him. A few weeks later, when it looked like he might live after all, she sent the boy into town to see if anyone was reported missing in the creek. He said only some wanted man, a Mr. Skraggs, but from the wanted poster, he was a lot younger than this man and had brown hair instead of gray, a straight nose instead of a crooked one, and was from Indiana, not Oregon.

They didn't tell anyone about the man. Who was there to tell? Ever since her man was killed in a feud with the neighbors, they didn't have no truck with them, nor the law. They kept to themselves and took care of themselves, her and Orville. And now Eddie. They took care of Eddie. And when he was well, he'd take care of them. She'd see to it.

She didn't believe in God no more, but—if she did—she'd think He'd sent this man to take the place of the one taken away. She could use a man.

Acknowledgments:

This novel grew out of a research project I participated in on the one-room schools of southwestern LaPlata County, Colorado. I need to thank the pioneers of LaPlata County for sharing their stories and memories at the Old School Days gathering at Fort Lewis Mesa School on July 9, 2005, and through letters, pictures, and interviews. While there are too many to mention each by name, special thanks must be given to Lila Greer whose reminiscences of Picnic Flat School provided the inspiration and some of the incidents in this book. Former teachers Nellie Oldfield Horvath, Emma Paulek Horvath, Carmen Cordell Wood, and Nora Malles also provided valuable information and inspiration.

Members of the Word Wranglers writers' group Clara Mae Schmitt, Cindy Greer, Barbara Kugle, Jane Westgaard, Clarice Schmid, LaVerne Pulliam, Barbara Lukow, Jeremy Robins, and Diana Schmitt provided valuable critiques. Other readers who also contributed their expertise included historian Dr. Duane Smith, Gay Smith, Chris Goold, Catherine Dougharty, Martha Schmitt, Jenny Coons, Janelle McQuitty, and Connie Peters.

Thanks also to the editorial staff at Western Reflections Publishing for their kind and thorough attention to my manuscript.

While the book is based on historical facts, the characters and setting are fictional. Any similarity to anyone living or dead is entirely coincidental.

If you enjoyed *Minta Forever*, you may like reading these other books from Western Reflections Publishing Co.:

Cochetopa Dreams by Carroll E. Allison

Father Struck It Rich by Evalyn Walsh McLean

Maggie's Way by Lucinda Stein

Bess by Carol Crawford McManus

Ida by Carol Crawford McManus

Alienation of Affection by Robert Hardaway